savage hate

SAVAGE HEARTS BOOK ONE

AMANDA RICHARDSON

Savage Hate
Amanda Richardson
Published by Amanda Richardson

www.authoramandarichardson.com

Editing by Nice Girl, Naughty Edits
Cover Design by Moonstruck Cover Design & Photography
Cover Photography by Wander Aguiar

author's note

Savage Hate is an enemies-to-lovers reverse harem romance. It is a spin-off of the Ruthless Royals duet, and takes place in the same world (with some crossover in later books).

While it does not end with a true cliffhanger, there are unanswered questions still to be resolved in book two and three, which release March 15, 2022 and May 10, 2022. You can preorder Savage Gods and Savage Reign here.

Please note the trigger warnings in the blurb, which is located on the next page.

As always, thank you for reading, and enjoy!

There are three names that have haunted me for ten years.

Silas, Damon, Jude.

I never wanted to come back to Greythorn, MA. And I never thought I'd see Silas Huxley, Damon Brooks, or Jude Vanderbilt again—especially not after what happened.

But here they are, in all of their grown, badass glory—brutal, tatted, muscular, and no longer the boys I knew at Ravenwood Academy—the boys I bullied relentlessly.

I made their life a living hell back then, so they plan on making my life a living hell now.

They're out for blood—*my* blood. Their ruthless thirst for revenge turns my skin to ice, and I soon discover just how savage and hateful they are.

But despite popular opinion, my life was never full of butterflies and sunshine. I've endured a hell of a lot worse than what they plan to do to me.

They may think I'm back in Greythorn with my tail between my legs, all battered and bruised—but what they've forgotten is that I am the original Queen of Ravenwood Academy.

And I refuse to be dethroned.

Savage Hate is full-length enemies-to-lovers/bully reverse harem romance. It is a spinoff of the Ruthless Royals duet, which does **not** have to be read first. It is book one of the Savage Hearts series, and while it doesn't end with a true cliffhanger, there will be unanswered questions. Book two will be releasing on March 15, 2022. It is advised to read them in order. ***Please note Savage Hate contains explicit language, bullying, needles, and violence. There are flashbacks of abuse/grooming/trauma. The series will have a HEA.**

To my smut lovers...

If you think this one is steamy, wait until book two.

**(I wasn't sure this would be the dedication, but I accidentally texted it to the group chat with my in-laws, so now you all have to live with my secondhand embarrassment).*

prologue

Silas

Ten Years Ago

I clench and unclench my fists, heat flaming my cheeks as the cacophonous laughter permeates the quad of Ravenwood Academy. Gathering my courage, I continue walking toward the locker room, aware of the hole that's now cut out of the front of my pants. I wish I had Damon's swagger, or Jude's composure, but instead, fury roils just beneath the surface of my skin as I shove the locker room doors open.

Enough.

I've had *enough.*

I grind my teeth and crack my neck as I walk to my row, unlocking my gym locker and grabbing a pair of P.E. shorts. Stepping out of my pants, I kick them away with too much force, and my foot slams into the metal of the locker.

"Fuck!" I shout, punching the locker a few times until my knuckles are bloody. "Fuck her," I mutter, kicking the locker again until it dents. "Fuck Lennon Rose." I wipe my nose and take a few steadying breaths before pulling my P.E. shorts on and sitting on the bench. Putting my face in my hands, I groan. How does she always find a way to humiliate me? How is it that she hasn't moved on to someone else? Why me? Why us?

I feel their presence before I hear them.

"People are already talking about the game later," Jude says, sitting down next to me. "By tomorrow, everyone will have forgotten."

I look up and watch as Damon paces in front of me. "You already know my thoughts on the subject," he growls, frustration contorting his features. "Revenge is the only answer. She may be more popular than us, but there are three of us and only one of her."

I sigh and rub my face, standing and grabbing my trousers from their place on the concrete floor.

"She's not worth it," I say morosely. "She thinks she can continue messing with me—that one day she'll break me, but she's wrong. She's just a stupid cunt who will go on to lead a miserable life."

"Exactly," Jude adds, handing me my backpack.

"Well, we could—"

"I said no," I answer, turning to Damon. I look between them, willing my features to remain neutral. "It was just a stupid fucking prank. We have one more month until we graduate. One month. And then we can get the fuck out of Greythorn."

And I never have to see Lennon Rose again.

I ball up my now ruined pants and toss them into the garbage, my fury returning when I think about the fact that everyone inadvertently saw my dick and nuts, thanks to the loose flap in my boxers. A faux pas on a normal day, but more so because Lennon fucking Rose and her minion thought it would be funny to cut a hole in my pants during P.E. class. Even funnier for her, I didn't notice until a few minutes after.

At least it wasn't freezing out, so there was no shrinkage happening. Not that anyone would care either way.

The three of us walk out of the locker room, and I ignore the snickers of passing students who haven't already forgotten what just happened. Jude and Damon head to their classes, and I walk alone to my last class of the day. One more class, and then we can head to Jude's house and chill with some beer and chips. And I can forget that today ever happened.

I tamp down the anger when I see Lennon sitting at the front of the room, her spine straight, her honey blonde hair falling down her back in loose waves. I look down at myself, at the gym shorts paired with the polo shirt. A few people raise their eyebrows as I sit down, and I swallow the insecurities that begin to rise to the surface.

My skinny legs.

My glasses.

My lack of muscle no matter how many hours I spend at the gym.

My messy hair.

I disregard the feeling of embarrassment at that last thought. Getting a haircut just isn't a priority, not with Ledger struggling in middle school. I'm his only parental figure since ours are missing in action, away at some religious conference or something. Grinding my jaw, I lean back and check my phone quickly. Between making our breakfast, packing our lunches, grocery shopping, cooking dinner, cleaning the house... I barely have time for homework, let alone a haircut.

My eyes bore into the back of Lennon's head.

She has *no idea* what my life is like, yet she uses her free time to torment me. Lennon Rose has a perfect house, a perfect life, an acceptance letter to Harvard... I try to tamp down the jealousy. I don't want to go to Harvard, but college is out of the question for me. I have to take care of Ledger and make sure he doesn't turn into a religious freak like our parents. But Lennon? She's an only child. She has everything and everyone at her beck and call. Not only do her parents own half of Greythorn's real estate, but everyone at Ravenwood Academy worships the ground she walks on, which is obvious since she was crowned prom queen last month.

Our teacher walks in and begins lecturing, and just as I'm about to look away from that glossy hair, she turns around, giving me a nasty little smile. Her ruby lips quirk upwards, and her deep, hazel eyes pin me with a defiant stare. Her eyes flick to my shorts and then back to my face, narrowing her eyes before snapping her head forward again, dismissing me by flicking her hair with her hand.

Evil.

She is evil incarnate.

A brat, and a bully.

And for some unknown reason, she's chosen me as her prey.

I clench my jaw and ignore her. Just as I pull out a notebook to take notes, Lennon raises her hand. Mr. Geary nods his head once, a look of unrelenting exhaustion on his face. I'm not the only person Lennon torments. She abuses everyone in her path, including poor, old Mr. Geary.

"Yes, Miss Rose?"

She straightens as she clasps her hands together on her desk—prim and proper.

"I just wanted to note that Mr. Huxley is not adhering to the dress code," she says sweetly. "He's wearing his P.E. shorts, which is against the rules," she adds, and everyone in the class begins to laugh. "If girls have to ensure our skirts aren't too short, surely the boys should be held to the same standard."

She cranes her neck to look back at me, a look of disgust on her face. I fight the heat that creeps up my neck, and the way my hands begin to shake.

One month.

One month.

One month.

I stand up and grab my things as renewed rage

flames through me. I've had enough of her shit, and surviving until graduation is going to need to be priority. I don't want any part of her sick games. I don't want to be her punching bag anymore.

"I'm leaving," I say to her as I walk down the aisle to the front of the classroom. I pass right by her before falling flat on my face, and the class erupts with a boom of laughter as I pull myself up, realizing the foot she stuck out to trip me.

"Oops," she taunts, cocking her head and smiling. "My bad."

My eyes don't leave hers, and I swear I see an inkling of fear in them as I let all of my hatred for her show on my face. Giving Mr. Geary a tight nod, I open the door forcefully and stalk down the hallway.

Like I said, evil incarnate.

One day, I will get my revenge.

One day, I will push Lennon Rose past her breaking point.

one

Lennon

Present

Slamming the taxi door shut, I shield my eyes against the summer sun, looking at the building before me. I reach down and pull my two suitcases onto the sidewalk and look around the familiar street, swallowing as a few people look me up and down. I pull my baseball hat lower on my head and stare at the address in front of me, comparing it to the text my mother sent through an hour ago. A text. First time back in Greythorn in ten years, and she sends a text. *Mother of the year award goes to Genevieve Rose...*

I sigh as I walk up to the building, and two doors greet me. One is made of glass, and it appears to lead to a tattoo parlor. The other is to the left, with white, peeling paint, and the address is scrawled on it haphazardly with a sharpie. Scowling, I enter the code from my mom's text and the door clicks open. I try and fail to gracefully get inside in one go, opting to bring in each large piece of luggage separately. By the time I get upstairs to the apartment landing, I've already been up and down the narrow staircase three times, and I'm panting as I enter the code for the door.

It swings open, and I groan when I see what's before me. It's a small studio apartment with a mattress on the floor, a small kitchenette, and a bathroom to my right. It's no bigger than a hotel room. There's a TV, a couch, and a small coffee table, and the décor could use some updating. I'm not sure anyone has stayed here in months. The smells of mildew and old food hit my nostrils, and I press my lips together as I drop my purse onto the dated, tile counter.

This is fine.

More than fine—it's free, which is all I can currently afford. I didn't know the shop downstairs had turned into a tattoo parlor. Last time I was here, it had been an old bookshop. That was one of the reasons my dad bought it a few years before he died—though I don't know what compelled him to eventually buy the whole building.

He loved books and reading. It was the one highlight of my childhood.

The *only* highlight.

I rub my chest and close my eyes, tears pricking my lashes. Inhaling deeply, I pull my phone out and let my mom know I've arrived.

For the next hour, I unpack and try to cram all of my shoes, bags, and clothes into the one dresser and small closet. When I'm done, I take inventory of the essentials—pots, pans, plates, cups, mugs, coffeemaker. It's pretty well-stocked, though the quality of cookware and bakeware is slightly lacking. I'm already itching to bake something, but I'll have to wait until I'm making money to buy the necessary ingredients. I make a list of things that need to be purchased, knowing it could be weeks, or months, before I can afford to do anything other than survive.

I lean against the counter and look around, biting my lower lip as I continue to rub my chest. It feels wrong to be back here, somehow. Wrong to be twenty-eight and living in a place my mom owns–and not even the house I grew up in, because it's currently being renovated.

Just a week ago, my life was so different. I had a plan, a life ahead of me. I had everything I'd ever wanted, everything I'd ever dreamt of. My life was supposed to lead to my happily ever after–a reprieve from my shitty childhood and adolescence.

Until it didn't.

Maybe that was the problem, maybe I expected too much. Maybe I dreamed a little *too* hard with the unattainable fairytale endings I'd planned out in my head. The first eighteen years were fucked up, but maybe the rest of my life would be okay, right?

Maybe that's why Wright did what he did.

I was too busy daydreaming to notice that my fiancé was sleeping with his executive assistant.

I was too busy daydreaming to realize that the townhouse we bought together wasn't actually mine in writing, and that I had no right to any of *our* money.

I always assumed we'd get married, have kids, and live the Upper East Side lifestyle I so coveted.

That was my problem. I was too distracted with the dream to see the reality. I was so eager to leave this place behind and live the life I always wanted... and look where that got me.

Back in Greythorn now, ten years older, with nothing to show for it.

I tug my shirt over my head and then slide my leggings and underwear off. Pulling the hair tie out of my hair, I walk to the shower and turn the handle, waiting for the hot water.

It doesn't come, so I grit my teeth and step into the cold stream, gasping as the frigid water hits my skin. I take the world's fastest shower and I'm shivering when I wrap the small, thin towel around my body. It's warm out, but my teeth are chattering. Pulling on some sweats and a t-shirt, I pad to the kitchen and find a takeout menu for the pizza place down the street. I don't have a ton of money left, but I have enough for essentials for about two weeks.

The thought is terrifying, and I ignore it altogether while I wait for the pizza to show up. It's barely past five in the evening, and I can already tell that I'll be settling in early tonight with trashy TV—just like I've done the last few nights at a motel since everything happened.

I've gotten good at distracting myself from my current reality.

The pizza arrives, and I eat the entire thing before climbing into the double bed. Checking my phone every few minutes, my heart sinks deeper into my empty chest when I realize my mom has no intention of texting me back anytime soon.

And even though my entire life was turned upside down last week, that fact makes me the saddest of all.

two

Lennon

A crash startles me out of a deep, peaceful sleep—the first restful sleep I've had in over a week. Heart racing, I throw the covers off and sit up in bed, looking around the small apartment. Muffled laughter sounds from the stairwell, or what sounds like the stairwell, and I walk over to the front door as I listen. Deep, male voices echo up to the second story, and I realize with a sinking feeling that they're not in the stairwell. They're downstairs, in the tattoo parlor. My eyes glance at the clock on the oven. 12:52.

Another crash sounds, and I let out a frustrated growl. Throwing a thick, oversized cardigan over my silky sleep dress, I grab my keys and open the door, walking down the concrete steps barefoot. I land heavily on each foot, anger fueling me as I shove the door to the street open, twisting to my left and glaring into the windows of the parlor. It's dark inside, and I squint as I put my face against the glass to peer inside.

Three men are sitting on the couch, beers in hand, laughing. They don't notice me at first, and I can't see them well enough to know if I recognize them. Greythorn is a nice area—and these guys don't look very nice. From what I *can* see, which isn't much, two of them appear to be inked up, and all of them are wearing black... that's about all I can ascertain.

I take a step back and peer at the sign swinging in the cool, late-night breeze.

Savage Ink.

The letters are wrapped around a hand drawn heart, and the *I* is a knife, poised to stab the middle of the heart. *Cool logo... not so cool people.*

Scowling, I step forward and knock on the front door, which appears to be locked. I see one of them get up to answer. Do they work here? Their ink says yes, but then again, the place doesn't seem open... the least they could do is be cordial. It sounds like they're smashing beer bottles against the wall.

My jaw is clenched as a man opens it. He cocks his head as he leans against the door frame, and I study his small smile, my words getting caught in my throat when I take him in. He's... gorgeous. I'm suddenly aware of my flimsy sleep dress, and I pull my cardigan together as I take in the two guys behind him. *Drunk.* They are drunk. I narrow my eyes at the man before me.

"Can you please, for the love of God, keep the noise

down?" I try to keep my tone even, but the annoyance is evident. "It's nearly one in the morning," I add, my eyes roving over his crystal blue ones.

He's young, about my age, with wavy, dark blonde hair that falls slightly in front of his face. His jawline is angular, cheekbones high… of Scandinavian descent, perhaps. Something about him is familiar. He's wearing a black thermal and black jeans. My eyes flick behind him again as two other guys meander over to the door.

"Who is it?" one of them asks. He pokes his head over the first guy's shoulder. "Oh."

This guy is the opposite of the first guy, with longer, messy, dark hair, dark eyes, and eyebrows that pin you to the spot with their intensity. Plus, he's a good six inches taller than the first guy. Massive, menacing, and terrifying.

A third guy pokes his head over the other's shoulder, and his eyebrows shoot up as he takes me in. He's the most beautiful of the trio, with shaggy, light brown hair, golden eyes, and pale skin. There's a chilling, predatory stillness about him. Something almost otherworldly.

"What are you doing here, Lennon?" the third guy asks, and my name on his lips startles me.

They must know me from high school, but I certainly don't remember any tall, muscular, tatted guys at Ravenwood.

"You know who I am?" I ask, looking between them.

The first guy hasn't taken his eyes off me, and his expression is now showing a mix of hatred and loathing. Narrowing his eyes, he steps off the landing so that he's right in front of me. *Too close to me.* I step back, but he takes another intimidating step forward. Tall—he's so tall. They all are. Suddenly, I'm acutely aware of the fact that I'm surrounded by three giant, strange men.

"Of course, we know who you are," the first guy growls. "Which is why, and I mean this with all of my heart, I am asking you to get the fuck out of here." His voice is so deep that I nearly feel it reverberating in my bones.

Before I can process his words, he turns around and slams the door in my face.

"What the hell," I whisper, shaking my head. Just as I turn to walk back upstairs, loud, heavy metal music begins to blast through the speakers.

Great.

I'm still shaking my head as I close my apartment door behind me. How did they know who I was? Why did they seem like they hated me? I have *zero* idea who they are. Perhaps I'd met them with Wright at some point? No... they weren't the kind of guys my ex-fiancé would socialize with...

My phone pings. It's past midnight, so I have no idea who could be trying to contact me, except...

Sighing, I open my mom's text.

Glad you're settled in. I'll be back this weekend and we can have lunch together.

Her casual lunch suggestion irritates me. For one, my life is falling to fucking pieces right now. Everything I once knew and loved is in tatters. I'm broke and alone, with no job or prospects for where to live, or how I'll afford to stay alive. Two, I'm her only child, and I haven't seen her since my father's funeral nearly two years ago.

Swallowing the lump in my throat, I walk to the kettle to make a pot of herbal tea. It's not like she's ever been the epitome of maternal warmth. She couldn't even find time in her schedule to welcome me back to Greythorn.

In the same week, I found out the house I *thought* I co-owned with Wright is actually not my house at all in the legal sense. And all those "friends" I'd made over the last few years? Gone at the first whisper of trouble. They were Wright's friends, after all. I didn't exactly blame them for choosing his side.

I had nothing, and no one.

A tear springs free from the corner of my eye, and I swipe at it angrily as the floor vibrates with the bass of the heavy metal.

Fuck this.

Fuck all of this.

Coming back to Greythorn was a terrible idea.

three

Silas

I disguise my shaking hands by jamming them into the pockets of my jeans. Nodding my head to the ridiculous music, I look over at Damon and Jude, who are casually playing a game of cards on the reception desk. Ignoring them, I walk over to the window, taking another sip of beer and watching the summer mist begin to cling to the town square and the park in the middle of it all.

Lennon Rose.

I never thought I'd see her again, but there she fucking was, in all her gorgeous glory. Because holy fuck, she definitely grew up. I suppose I did, too. But Lennon? Tall, blonde, probably a little too thin—which explained the bags under her eyes, and the fact that she was back in Greythorn. Her voice… it brought back memories of our time at Ravenwood Academy, and the last time I saw her at the graduation party.

Last I heard, she was going to marry some rich fuck in New York. I was looking forward to never seeing her again. My life was here now, despite the haunting memories. *Despite* how she'd tainted and tarnished my adolescence. I'd left Boston against my will, but I've made do since being back, discovering that Greythorn was never the issue–*Lennon Rose* was the issue.

But now she was here to shit all over everything, just like she always did.

I can't help the fury that roils under my skin at the memory of graduation night, because fuck her, and her perfect legs, and her perfect tits. Double fuck the delicate, heart-shaped face and the long, shapely legs.

But no.

She almost fucking ruined my life, and as she spoke, as she *whined* about the noise, I couldn't help but be transported back to that time.

For four years, she made my life Hell.

For four years, I dreamed of strangling her. Of enacting revenge so great, she'd never even look my way again.

Maybe now was my chance.

four

Lennon

I wake up late the next morning, and my head is pounding for coffee. Groaning, I roll over and instinctively reach for Wright. The realization of what happened in the last week catapults into me with such shock and force that I pull the duvet over my head and scream when I realize this is now my reality.

How did I get here? Living in the apartment my mother rents out month to month. Back in my hometown. No job, no close friends... nothing. If I had the money, I would've preferred Italy or Bali. Lesson learned—always have access to your own money. Because when your cheating fiancé locks the bank accounts and moves things around, leaving you with $350 to your name?

Yeah, it's a slap in the face. And a wake-up call. The lawyers I called didn't seem to have any answers for me, either. Even though it was my money, I didn't have a job or an official income, so it would be hard to explain how I'd accrued thousands of dollars in cash selling cupcakes to Wright's friends.

Sighing, I climb out of bed and throw on some jeans and a t-shirt. I don't bother with my hair, instead pulling it up into a high, tight bun. Slipping into my sandals, I grab my purse and head out in search of some coffee. As I walk down the stairs, I listen for any noises at the tattoo parlor, but it seems to be empty now. When I glance inside a second later, it's dark, and I don't see anyone sitting on the couch like last night.

Good.

By the time I have a hot coffee and a warm croissant in my hand, I'm a happy camper. I take a seat at one of the benches overlooking the central park. I've always loved this park, despite loathing this town growing up. It's lively, with everyone walking through it from one side of town to the other, and the restaurant behind me always has people sitting outside at tables for brunch. Especially with beautiful weather like this.

I didn't bother to text my mom back last night, so instead I text Mindy, my one and only friend. She lives in the next town over, never having really left the area after high school. Married with two kids, she's the only person from Greythorn that I've kept in touch with, and I ask if she wants to get a coffee sometime this week. I can't afford to take her to lunch, but I can buy her a coffee. She responds almost instantly, and we make a plan for this Monday.

Standing, I throw my trash away and stretch my arms above my head as I look around. I *want* to go back to the apartment and crawl underneath my covers. I *want* to order junk food and binge Netflix shows until my eyes sting and my stomach hurts. I feel so raw, so vulnerable, that maybe I should do those things. But, where would that get me? No, I need to move forward and get my life together.

I've had a week to wallow.

Now it's time to get things done.

The first thing I do is go grocery shopping, which is not easy being in a town where the mean income per capita is six figures. I manage to score some pasta on sale. Even though it will be a while before I can afford to eat meat, I manage to stick to my budget for the week. I hope to have a job soon, and if I can stretch my money for a couple of weeks, I can survive on pasta, bread, and baked beans.

Forget baking, too. That'll have to come later.

I ignore the way my eyes sting and my throat aches when I think about how different my life is now, and instead head back to the apartment to unload my food and necessities. My eyes shift to the left when I get to my building. Thankfully, Savage Ink is still empty, and I carry on up the stairs. When I'm finished unloading my groceries, I make myself some eggs and scarf an apple before going on a walk through town.

Ten years. Ten years since I've been back in Greythorn. Ten years since I was crowned prom queen, valedictorian, *and* most likely to succeed by the student body. I swallow when I think about what those students would say about me now—how they would perceive my life… and my fall from glory. I quicken my pace through the dense forest in the middle of the park.

I veer left and begin to walk toward the house I grew up in. The house which was currently being renovated and one of the reasons why I was staying in the apartment. When I get to our house, I breathe out a sigh of relief. It still looks the same—large, grand, three stories with tall, Edwardian windows. Ours was one of the oldest houses in Greythorn, dating back to the 1700s. My dad came from old money, as do most of the people who live here, but this house had been in our family for generations. I pause in front of the front door, remembering my childhood. Remembering the nights I went to bed hungry, or the nights my chest ached from disappointment and loneliness.

Everyone always thought I'd had the perfect life, but in reality, my parents didn't parent me. They never did. I was often left by myself or with a nanny. It wasn't a terrible childhood, just barren of warmth and comfort. I wrap my arms around my body and begin to walk back to the apartment.

As I round the corner, I notice the door of Savage Ink is propped open. Walking slowly, I let out a sigh of relief when I see a woman with long, dark hair sitting behind a desk, her phone in her hand. I step over the threshold and smile.

"Hi," I say, attempting to give her a warm smile.

Her eyes flick to my face in surprise. “Do you have an appointment?”

I shake my head. “No, I’m not here to...” I look around. I don’t have any tattoos, even though a small part of me has always wanted to get one. “I just moved into the apartment upstairs. I wanted to introduce myself.”

She perks up and stands. “Oh! That’s exciting. I’m Lola,” she croons, holding her hand out.

“Lennon,” I reply, shaking her hand and smiling as I look around. “I met... I’m not sure who I met last night, but there were three of them and they were very tall.”

She huffs a laugh. “Oh, Silas, Damon, and Jude?” The familiar names slam through me one at a time, and my horror must be evident on my face because she goes on to elaborate. “Don’t mind them. They’re just grumpy old men, even though they might look a bit mean.”

I swallow and feel the blood leaving my face. “Silas... Huxley?”

She nods once. “That’s the one.”

Silas Huxley.

The guy I humiliated in front of our classmates on graduation night. The guy I nearly killed, if the rumors were correct. *Guys.* I nearly killed all three of them.

And Damon Brooks? Jude Vanderbilt? *Fuck.* That’s who I saw last night? I begin to piece it together—the recognition on their faces, the anger, telling me to fuck off...

It all makes sense now.

“I knew them in high school,” I mumble, looking

around the parlor. "I never would've pegged them as tattoo guys..."

She laughs again and resumes her seat behind the desk. "They had a place in Boston. It was famous—they're the best in the area. But Silas had to move back home after... well, you know."

I shake my head. "What?"

I don't know much about Silas—not really. He had a younger brother, and his parents were total freaks. He was constantly ridiculed in high school, especially since anyone who visited his home also knew about the creepy chapel in the basement. That tall, muscular man with crystal blue eyes, the man I saw last night... *that* was Silas? The last time I laid eyes on him, he was no taller than me, skinny, and small. He'd had thick black glasses and his pants were always too short. My heart clenches when I think of what I used to do to him—what I used to say to him.

Get the fuck out of here.

No wonder he hates me.

"His parents aren't doing so well." She looks me up and down. "Were you all... close in high school?"

I bark out a laugh. "Not at all."

She gives me a soft smile. "What brings you back to Greythorn?"

I look at her before my eyes skim the rest of the shop. Metal jewelry is laid out neatly in glass cases. A brown chesterfield sits near the front desk, and all kinds of taxidermized animals line the walls, which are covered with gorgeous skull and flower wallpaper. There are Victorian portraits in gilded frames, old fashioned sconces, and three black leather station chairs for the tattooing. I wonder if all three guys are tattoo artists? Jude didn't have any tattoos... that I could see.

"It's a long story," I answer, glancing over at the front door and then back at her as I sigh. "You wouldn't happen to know of any job openings anywhere, would you?"

Lola perks up. "Actually, I do. We're hiring a full-time receptionist. I'm only here on Friday's now, and the guys can't keep up. They need help most nights with things like scheduling, paperwork..." She looks me up and down. "It's easy, and I can train you."

I swallow as I take in her inked arms and septum piercing. She's gorgeous, with long black hair, golden skin, brown eyes, and the most alluring lips I've ever seen.

"Do I need tattoos to work here?"

She bursts out laughing and shakes her head. "Absolutely not. Jude is one of the artists and he has zero tattoos, so there's already a precedent."

I laugh. "I'll think about it." I take a few steps backwards. "Thank you, by the way."

She nods once. "You're welcome, Lennon. It's nice to meet you. Just drop your resume here later, okay?"

I nod. "Okay. Thanks again."

I head upstairs, smiling and shaking my head. Working at Savage Ink? With Silas Huxley, Damon Brooks, and Jude Vanderbilt?

What could possibly go wrong?

Damon

"You *what*?" I ask, seething.

Lola looks between the three of us. "I—I offered her the receptionist job?"

"And why," Silas asks slowly, his jaw ticking, "would you ever do that?"

Lola furrows her brows. "I don't understand. Don't you know her from high school?"

Jude chuckles lightly, and I release my clenched fists. "Yes, we knew her," I reply, my tone menacing. "She was a total cunt."

Lola flinches as she begins to sort through paperwork. "Well, you better work it out amongst yourselves unless you want to keep turning business away." She looks at all of us again. "I think you should hire her. She's the first person to inquire in over a month." She pins me with a death stare, and I know in an instant that we're about to lose this battle. No one goes up against Lola Gonzalez and wins. "Or, you could learn how to use this damn scheduler," she finishes, a bite to her voice as she nods to the computer. "I'm sick of coming in here once a week and having to clean up your goddamn messes."

Jude's lips twitch, and he walks over to his station, hanging his leather jacket on the coat rack. He's been mostly quiet about our new upstairs neighbor. Then again, he's not one to show his true feelings to anyone–even us.

"I'd rather this place go under than hire Lennon Rose as our new receptionist," Silas says bitterly. "Find someone else." And then he walks off to his station, stewing in his anger.

Lola looks up at me from her seat, her lips puckered in displeasure. "Find me someone else and I'll happily hire them," she counters. "But honestly, if you don't, this place may very well go under, and everything you've worked for will go down the shitter."

Jude lets out a laugh from where he sits, sanitizing the area for his first client.

"It could've been anyone else," I counter. "Literally, *anyone* but Lennon Rose."

Lola frowns and looks over at Silas. "She seems very nice. Maybe you should all grow up and get over whatever grudge you have against her. It's been, what? Eight years? Nine?"

"Ten," I correct.

She swings her head to face me. "Okay, ten. Even

more of a reason to let it go." She gives us all the finger as she walks to the back and closes the bathroom door.

Jude walks over to where I'm standing, and the look on his face...

"No." I already know what he's thinking, and it's a horrible idea. "Absolutely not, man."

He crosses his arms and brushes his lip with his thumb. "You don't even know what I was going to say."

I burst out laughing. "Yeah fucking right. I've known you your whole fucking life."

"Come on," he whines, a twisted, little smile playing on his lips. Everyone thinks he's the innocent one—the one without tattoos, the face of an angel, the *quiet* one. But he's the sickest of us all, and I know he's suggesting one of his depraved games. "Let's hire her and fuck with her a bit. Give her a taste of her own medicine."

Silas stills at his station, before he slowly turns to face us. "What are you suggesting?" he asks, and I shake my head.

"No," I repeat. "I'm not fucking around with the future of this shop. Let's just hire someone else and get on with it."

Silas stands and saunters over to the front of the parlor to where we're standing. Normally, I'm the psychotic one, so the fact that they're both considering this...

His eyes dart between the two of us. "Fuck with her how?" he asks Jude, and I spin around to face him.

"She's right, you know. It's been ten years. Forgive and forget. Time to move on. We don't have to hire her."

Silas's eyes find mine, and they narrow ever so slightly. "Forgive and forget? Do you remember graduation night?"

Jude nods, and I wince. "Yeah, man, but I mean—"

"What do you all want for lunch?" Lola asks, startling us as she walks back over to the desk and plops down. "I was going to get a burrito. Want me to get four?"

Silas just looks at Jude, and I know in an instant that it's been decided by the way his lips curve upwards.

Fuck me.

"Sure. Sounds great, Lo," Silas says, his voice faraway. "And by the way, you're right. Time to move on from high school. Why don't you give her a call." He gestures to her resume. "Tell Lennon Rose she has the job."

Double fuck me.

six

Lennon

I glance at my reflection in the mirror before smoothing my hair. I'm not exactly sure what to wear for my first day at Savage Ink, so I opted for something comfortable and *me*—ripped, high-waisted skinny jeans and a black tank top. Wright would've hated everything about it, which makes me smile as I style my hair in long, loose waves. I apply a bit of makeup and then pull on my black boots.

I can do this.

They are just three people I went to high school with.

There's nothing special about them.

Silas, Damon, and Jude had no idea what my life was like back then, but hopefully we can all make amends now that we're adults. I need a job, and they need a receptionist... it's time to move on. I grab my purse and phone, seeing it's almost six, and then I head downstairs.

It's still light out when I push the door of Savage Ink open. Lola is sitting at the desk, on her phone, and she's spinning from side to side in her rolling chair.

"Hi!" she welcomes me, standing. "I can't stay long," she adds quickly, looking down at her phone. "But I can show you the ropes before I go. It's easy, so it should only take twenty minutes." Her phone buzzes. "Fuck, one second." She answers and turns around. "Hi, sweetie. What's wrong?" She looks over her shoulder and gives me an apologetic look. "Ah, I see. Did you ask Vivienne to share her toys?" She pauses. "Okay, sweetie. I will be home soon." She hangs up and sighs. "Sorry, I have a very strong-willed toddler who's at her friend's house right now," she says, shaking her head. "My partner is a firefighter, and he works nights, hence why I can only work Fridays."

I nod and smile. "I appreciate you taking the time to train me."

She smirks. "Trust me. You're doing *me* a favor. I come in every Friday to a billion post-it notes because these dolts never learned how to use QuickBooks or Microsoft."

I laugh, but then my nerves get the best of me.

I've never used those things, either–unless you count memorizing cookie and cake recipes, and spending all day perfecting the perfect brownie. To give myself some credit, I do know my way around a professional stand mixer... but that is about as far as my real-world knowledge goes. College ended six years ago. And I never learned any of this shit. Any real-world experience I *should've* gotten was always taken care of by Wright or someone in his family, and they swooped in right after college.

I don't know anything about having a job. My resume says otherwise, though—that I helped Wright and his father at their firm for a few years after we graduated. But that was an embellishment. I only helped to decorate it, and by always ensuring the front desk was stocked with baked treats.

I wince a bit when I think about that. About how he had me cooped up in our penthouse for years without even realizing it. He constantly threw money at me for baking accessories, baking courses, fancy cookbooks... and I was too distracted with measuring and fondant to really take a closer look at what my life had become.

Lola gestures for me to take a seat at the second chair she's pulled up to the large iMac computer. She tells me how to log into the scheduling program, how to track expenses, how to work the phone system and answer emails. Everything is online now. There is a cleaner that comes twice a week, and the equipment supplier that comes once a week.

She then goes into each of the guy's styles, so if someone calls and wants something done, I can refer them to the right person. She shows me a book of pictures of their work, and I flick through, amazed. They're all incredible artists, having created some of the best tattoos I've ever seen.

Silas's style is very fine. He specializes in single needles, and his work is largely of nature, landscapes, flowers, and drawings. It's stunning and delicate, and he also has a lot of experience with gorgeous typography.

Damon's style is more traditional–heavy on the black ink, lots of calf and sleeve tattoos, and things a first-timer would get, like symbols and motifs. He has a surprisingly feminine touch, including lots of pink, purple, and blue. Lots of color in general, whereas Silas stays mostly in the black and grey arena.

And Jude? He's a true artist, one that recreates famous paintings, portraits, and large-scale masterpieces. It's all extraordinary, with swathes of color that look like true brush strokes and abstract drawings. The attention to detail in his work is breathtaking.

She then goes on to explain the jewelry and piercing station. I try not to squirm in my seat. I'm not exactly a huge fan of blood, which is funny because I'm working in a place full of needles.

The last thing she shows me are the social media pages for Savage Ink, and the kinds of images she typically posts. They're not super active, but it's something Lola likes to try to engage with a few times a week.

My head is spinning by the time she gathers her things. I try not to sound desperate when I ask if she'll be back tomorrow, but she shakes her head.

"No, but if you need anything, just give me a ring." She smiles and hands me a business card. "I bake cakes on the side, and my number is on there."

"You're a baker?" I ask, trying not to sound too eager. "Me too."

She quirks her lips to the side. "That's cool. I'm trying to open a bake shop, but I'm still saving up," she explains. "If I ever do it, maybe I can snatch you away from here to come work with me."

I laugh. "You won't have to snatch me. I'll leave willingly."

She smiles. "Mmmhmm. Give them a chance. They're good guys." Looking around, she nods once and sets a spare key on the desk. "They want the doors open at six, but their lazy asses don't show up until seven." I swallow, and she tilts her head as she smiles. "You'll be fine here," she yells over her shoulder, walking out. I'm not sure if she's talking to me, or to herself.

And then she's gone.

I familiarize myself with the computer, checking out the calendar for tonight. It's fully booked, and all three guys have appointments starting at seven, which is only fifteen minutes away. Sipping on some water, I text my mom about lunch and confirm with Mindy about our coffee date tomorrow. I'm just about to turn on some music when Silas walks through the door, stopping completely when he sees me.

In the light of the studio, I can already tell the last ten years did him some amazing favors. In fact, I can't even see the guy I used to know in his face at all. It's like he's a completely different person. I would almost believe he was if it weren't for the look of pure hatred on his face. And his eyes–I'll never forget how his crystal blue eyes always seemed to bore right down into the depths of my soul. He's wearing a grey t-shirt and dark jeans, and his muscled arms are covered in black ink. His blonde hair is falling over one side of his forehead, and his pouty lips are ticked downward as he studies me. Standing stock-still, his eyes flick down my body unabashedly, appraising me. He must not like what he finds, because his eyes meet mine again and he looks away quickly, unimpressed.

"Lennon," he says, a bite to his voice.

"Hi, Silas," I reply softly, as kind as I can be.

He just stalks off without saying another word. My cheeks heat as I look over to where he's setting up his station for his first appointment. I wait for him to look up, but he never does.

I answer a phone call five minutes to seven, telling the person on the other end of the line that they're all booked up tonight. Silas's head jerks up at that, and I wait for him to reprimand me, but he only scowls and hunches over his workstation.

Damon and Jude walk in a minute later, and unlike Silas, they both nod at me. No smiles. No warmth. But at least I get a nod of acknowledgement. They go over to their respective stations and begin to prepare. I didn't expect a warm welcome from any of them–not after what happened–but none of them even look back at me. Not until the first client walks through the door.

She's young, in her late teens, most likely. She seems a little nervous as she takes the studio in, and as her eyes adjust to the scene before her, she saunters up to me. I smile and get her checked in—ID confirmed, paperwork filled out, and deposit paid, all in a matter of ten minutes. I'm almost proud of myself as she takes a seat to wait for Damon to greet her. When he does, they walk to his station together. He remains professional, never once acting weird when she rolls her pants down a few times and exposes her bare hip.

The rest of the hour goes similarly—clients walk in, and I handle everything up until the artists walk them back to their chairs. When they're finished, the guys offer them beer, a snack, whatever they want. I'm starting to realize that it's an experience getting tattooed by these guys. They're kind, they're inviting, but most importantly, they make you feel like you're the only person in the room for that hour.

When their clients finish, I go over aftercare with all of them, and then I send them on their way with a little care package of antibacterial soap, unscented lotion, and a sticker that says *I got Savaged*. It's strange to think that these tattoos will probably be a part of these people's lives forever, and I wonder if the guys ever think about that. About the fact that they've left their mark on so many people walking around in the world.

I don't have very long to contemplate it though, because a few seconds later, Silas marches over to me and slaps a bucket of cleaning supplies and rubber gloves on the desk.

I look up at him questioningly. "What's this?"

He shrugs, and when his eyes meet mine, something

wrathful sweeps over his expression, darkening his pupils.

"When you're not doing paperwork, you're cleaning the bathroom."

I look around. It's not as busy anymore, but people are still regularly coming in for appointments.

"What—I—Lola said there were cleaners that come twice a w—"

"Not anymore," he cuts me off sternly. Giving me a monstrous smile, he cocks his head. "I'd double-glove if I were you, princess."

I grind my jaw as he walks away without further explanation. Grabbing the bucket, I walk to the bathroom since there's a lull of clients at the moment. After snapping the two pairs of gloves on, I look around and begin with the worst part—the toilet. It's not dirty per se, but I definitely didn't dress for cleaning toilets, nor did I expect it. I breathe through my mouth as I scrub the bathroom down from top to bottom. I check the front area periodically and help with any new clients that wander in, and in under an hour, I manage to turn an average bathroom into one worthy of a spotless, spa-like experience. While looking around for a final touch, I'd found some old fabric flowers, a vintage vase, and a candle, which really enhanced the vibe as well.

Walking back out, feeling accomplished, I set the cleaning supplies next to Silas's station. He's in the middle of tattooing a snake on a woman's ankle, his brows furrowed in concentration. Watching him work, noticing the way he grips the tattoo gun firmly with a gloved hand, his other set of strong fingers gently dabbing the ink...

I swallow as my stomach flutters. His eyes snap to mine, and his lips press together in a slight grimace as he blinks a few times before looking back down. Turning to walk away, my body stills when his voice cuts through the buzzing of the tattoo guns.

"Did you mop the floor?"

I have to actively *try* not to clench my fists. "Yes," I hiss, crossing my arms and turning to face him. "I also cleaned the walls, scrubbed the base of the toilet, and swapped out the hand towel for a new one."

His face remains blank as he hovers over his client. "Great. Can you please grab us some dinner?"

My hands automatically curl at my sides, flexing. "Am I the receptionist, or your personal assistant?" The words leave my mouth before I realize it, but I don't really care. This wasn't in Lola's job description, and it's now apparent that this job is a way for the guys to get vengeance on whatever grudge they still hold against me from high school.

Silas's bright blue eyes slice to mine, and he calmly turns his tattoo gun off and sets it down, murmuring something to his client. My eyes flick to Damon and Jude, who just give me furtive glances. They're not here to help me, or back me up. These guys come as a set, and it's crystal-clear who's side they would take in a standoff. Snapping his gloves off, Silas stands up and sets them down calmly—*too* calmly. His boots reverberate through the wood floors with every step, and when he gets to where I'm standing, I can smell his aftershave.

God, he is gorgeous. I know it probably makes me sound shallow, but talk about a glow up...

Swallowing hard, I look up into those blue irises, feeling dizzy all of a sudden. His jawline is sharp, his cheeks angular, and his lips? Totally bitable. He has short, dark blonde scruff with a hint of grey in the middle of his chin, which somehow adds to his allure. He crosses his arms, pushing his muscles up as they strain against the fabric of his t-shirt. *Like, damn...* what has Silas Huxley been eating these past ten years? Pure protein powder? What kinds of workouts does he do? I can't reconcile the man before me with the gangly boy I taunted for the entirety of my adolescence.

"If you have a problem being here, feel free to leave. I have other people who want this job." He studies me, waiting for me to walk out. Waiting for me to *break.* Waiting to prove that I can't handle this.

But the joke's on them, because this is a piece of cake compared to some parts of my childhood.

I think of the $290 I have to my name—the money that has to sustain me, or else I'll go hungry. I'd like to think my mom wouldn't let that happen, but history says otherwise. I'm already a failure, but at least one with a job that'll allow me to pay for my own place and get back on my feet.

I *need* this job, even if it means being Silas Huxley's little bitch.

"Fine," I concede sweetly. "I'll get you all some dinner."

His brows twitch ever so slightly. He must be wondering why I'm still here. But I won't ever give him the satisfaction of leaving.

Reaching into his back pocket, he pulls out a wad of cash, handing it to me. "We like the pizza place on the corner. Get yourself something, too." I take the cash, opening my mouth to say thanks, but he continues. "When you get back, the garbage cans out back really need to be hosed off."

As he walks away, it takes everything inside of me—every ounce of willpower—not to tell him to fuck off.

Instead, I think of Wright.

The whole way to the pizza place, I think of how he ruined everything by sleeping with his assistant, and for the rest of the night, I have to actively hold the tears back.

seven

Jude

I study Lennon as she types on the computer, my gaze flitting between her and my client. Another day, another fucking butterfly tattoo. I swear to God, half the population must have a butterfly permanently etched onto their skin at the rate we tattoo the insect on people.

"I like it," the woman before me says. She's beautiful, with dark hair and hazel eyes. Too young for me, but it's hard not to notice. It doesn't matter. I have not and will never mix business with pleasure. It's something we all agreed upon when we opened Savage Ink.

Damon and I were originally here just to support Silas, and we wanted to get the shop up and running before returning to Boston. But that plan is looking like it's happening less and less every day.

We've been in Greythorn for two years. Our time

spent in Boston is hazy now, and even though we go back a couple of times a month to check on Ignite Ink, the sister studio to Savage, I can't help but miss the bustle of the city. Being back in the town we all grew up in hasn't been thrilling, but we're here for Silas. We're a unit, in more ways than one.

I glance over at Damon as I get my client seated comfortably in the chair and we go over what will happen. His eyes connect with mine, and he nods once in understanding. She's a skin virgin—what we call people new to tattoos. Some people cry, some people don't seem affected at all, some people grit their teeth... and some people experience pleasure. It's one of the reasons I love inking people. I like to see the spectrum of reactions, because it can go any number of ways.

It's probably why I only have one tattoo. I'm not a sadomasochist for no reason.

My gaze falls back to Lennon as she squints at the screen. So far, she's taken everything Silas has thrown at her in stride. The bathroom bullshit, the pizza, the garbage cans. She returned from out back looking green in the face, but she didn't say anything—just washed her hands and got back to work. Maybe it's better to ease her in, anyway.

I'm trying to find her weak spot. Her fatal flaw.

Because when I do, I am going to expose it.

And I am going to break her.

For everything she did.

To me.

To Damon.

But mostly to Silas.

I smile when I think of what that pretty little face will look like once I do—once *we* do. Because that's our plan.

Push Lennon Rose as far as she'll go.

Beware the fury of a patient man, and beware the wrath of three.

eight

Lennon

Ten Years Ago

I pucker my lips in the mirror, smacking them a few times despite the sticky, clear lip gloss. Mindy is getting ready next to me, and music plays from her iPod as we sing along. I've had an ache in my chest all day. An overarching, hollow sense of dread and disappointment. I glance at the homemade snacks Mindy's mom placed out for us, wondering if she or Mindy noticed how many I'd eaten. Swallowing thickly, I continue staring at my reflection, wondering who will be at the party tonight.

"I heard Noah was going to ask you out tonight," Mindy says, looking at me with a huge grin.

I laugh. "Yeah, right. Like he thinks he has a chance." Secretly, I hope he does, but I'd never admit that out loud. We've been dancing around each other for months.

She shakes her head as she dabs on bright pink eyeshadow. "I still can't believe you'll be in Cambridge while I go to Greythorn University."

"I'm a forty-five-minute drive away," I chide, and she giggles. "It's not like I'm moving across the country."

"I know, but it's still weird that we won't be neighbors anymore."

I look around Mindy's room. She's right, and for a moment, I panic. I have a full scholarship to Harvard, and that includes a meal plan, but I can't discount the fact that Mindy and her parents are the only reason I've survived since they moved to Greythorn while we were in elementary school. If Mindy's parents suspect the neglect I encounter at home, they've never outright said anything. They invite me over for dinner most nights, and Mindy's mom, who doesn't work, volunteers to drive me around quite a bit.

My cheeks heat. *They must know.*

I walk back to the bed, glancing at my phone. It's a little past eight, and Noah is throwing an epic graduation party for the seniors. I change into my sparkly dress and matching heels, and Mindy helps me curl the back of my long blonde hair. I tell myself I look good even though I don't believe it. There are so many things I would change about my body. So many things I would change about my *life.*

One step at a time...

One day, I will have the perfect life. I won't be living in Greythorn under my parent's roof, and I can take charge of what *I* want–and not what's expected of me.

One day, I won't have to deflect and redirect by being rude, just so that people won't see the person hurting on the inside.

By the time we get into Mindy's Lexus, I'm shaking with anticipation.

"Who do you think will be there?" Mindy squeaks, and I can tell she's excited because her knees are bouncing energetically.

I shrug. "Probably everyone."

"Yeah, but, like... *everyone* everyone?"

I groan. "Noah would not have invited the dork storks, Mind."

She smirks and takes a sip of her soda. "Even if they dare to make an appearance, at least we never have to see them again after tonight."

I squirm in my seat, the hurt from today—from my parents not even showing up to my graduation ceremony—begins to balloon in my chest.

"If they show up, they will pay," I respond automatically.

The words feel good—great, even. I can never let him have the upper hand. Never let him win, or think he knows the *real* me.

So, I keep him and his little dork friends in their place.

It's the only way to survive without losing control completely.

"I still don't know why you're such a bitch to them." Mindy laughs. "Have you ever considered being nice?"

I look down. She's never tried to stop me, and that

tells me all I need to know about her approval of my behavior, so I don't answer her. I never do. It hurts too much to admit the truth to myself, so I do everything in my power to keep the upper hand. It would be mortifying if people knew I lived on ramen and whatever free food I could get, and there are weeks when I don't even have shampoo for my hair. I can't even imagine the humiliation on top of everything else going on in my life. I've seen the looks Silas and his friends throw my way. *Pity.* I can never let them dwell on it for too long—can never let them see what my life is really like.

Two months until I leave for Harvard...

Pulling up to Noah's gigantic house, I sigh as I get out of the car. People face me and watch as I walk up the driveway. I keep my eyes forward, not daring to meet anyone's gaze. Most of the time, I just want to be left alone. Why can't anyone see that?

The music is already loud enough to make the front door vibrate as I push it open. The large house is overflowing with people, and I do my best to ignore the cacophony of voices yelling over the music. Sliding past sweaty bodies, I slowly make my way through the crowd with Mindy. A couple of guys hoot and holler at us, but we ignore them as we search for Noah. We finally find him in the kitchen, drinking out of a red cup and talking to some sophomore. I roll my eyes. Noah is a senior at Greythorn University, so I know for a fact that this bitch is way too young for him.

The instant she sees me making a beeline for Noah, she squeaks and walks away, and I smile victoriously.

"Hi," I croon, throwing my arms around Noah's neck. "Great party."

Noah smiles. "Thanks, Len. Wanna go somewhere a little quieter?"

I feel Mindy nudge my ribs, and I nod, following him up the stairs. Noah plays football, and we met through mutual friends at one of his parties last spring. He's older and forbidden, and even though I'm only seventeen, I know I'm ready to be his girlfriend. He's hot, but I can't really have any sort of serious conversation with him—he's not the brightest bulb. Still, a girl like me can't be choosy.

Nobody else wants to date me.

They're all busy hating me.

He pulls me into a dark bedroom and closes the door. I giggle with surprise as his lips find mine, and he moves us to the bed against the left side wall. My eyes slowly take in my surroundings as they adjust to the dark, and then I gasp and pull away.

"Wait," I whisper, touching my lips. "Are you sure you want to..." I trail off. "At a party?"

Noah grins and nods. "Why not? It's your fucking graduation day, Lennon."

It doesn't matter to him. Noah Adelmann isn't a virgin like me. He dated Darya Vernon for two years, even though she was underage, too. I ignore the nagging feeling that it's not right for a twenty-two-year-old to be dating a sixteen-year-old... because that's how old I was when we met. All that being said, there's *no way* he's still a virgin. Tonight doesn't matter to him. It's just another night, another girl, another conquest. And while my self-loathing goes deep, it doesn't go *that* deep. My virginity is the one thing I can keep for myself. The one thing I can use against people.

My secret weapon.

I press a hand against his chest and sigh. "Not here, Noah. Not like this. Maybe we can go on a date this weekend or something, get to know each other a little better?"

The truth is, this terrifies me–letting him in even a little bit. I am stalling, and he knows it, but I can't help it. My hands shake as I push him away a little harder.

His nostrils flare, and his handsome face contorts into something angry. Something cruel and sinister that I haven't seen from him before.

"Are you fucking kidding me? You tease me for, what? An entire year? I bring you coffee, I buy you flowers, and I even send you videos of my... member." He chuckles darkly. "Are you really going to lie and tell me you didn't like seeing pictures of my cock?"

I swallow. He'd started sending them last summer.

I was only sixteen at the time.

Just a special secret between you and me...

"Is this because of Mindy?" he asks, his voice growing more vicious.

I scoff. "What does Mindy have to do with anything?"

He shrugs, taking a step closer. "I don't like how she makes you think."

Sighing, I shake my head. This is always a fight that

we have. Mindy loves Noah and his friends, yet Noah is convinced she's the reason we haven't had sex. I keep telling him I'm waiting for him to make it official, but he never does.

"You sound ridiculous," I chide, laughing. "I just don't want to lose my virginity in a bedroom at a party."

He rubs his lips and looks down at me. "Baby, come on. This is totally normal. You don't understand because you're so inexperienced." I wince at his words. He's not wrong, and it hits me right in the gut. Insecurity washes over me.

"I've done things with other guys," I hiss, pushing him away.

"Lennon, you *know* me. You've seen my cock. No one has a good first experience, but I can definitely try to make yours the best it can be."

"No," I reply, twisting around. Before I can walk away, Noah grabs my arm, pulling me into him.

"No one else understands what we have, baby. Are you really going to get me all riled up, and then turn me down at my own party? I thought we were friends." My mind is screaming at me to go, to run, to get away. Sure, I know Noah, but this? There's something in his eyes as he looks down at me that makes my heart beat faster, and not in a good way. "You do realize that I could have any girl here, right? Even that sophomore who was eye-fucking me. You're not special. You should be lucky that an older guy like me is going to make your first time memorable."

"I—"

Noah's hand goes over my mouth, and I scream as he presses me against the bed.

"Isn't this what you want?" he snarls from behind me. "Sending me your selfies with little fucking heart eyes," he growls. "You fucking want this. But I think you're too young to realize it, so how about we play a game?"

I shake my head and try to shove his hand off my face, but he's so much bigger than me.

"What we have is special. No one else understands. Especially not your friends," he murmurs, his hand roving to my bare thighs and up between them. I squeeze my legs shut.

"If it would make you feel better, we can keep this a secret. Just between you and me."

I cry against his hand, clawing at his arm, his body, trying to get away...

"Get your fucking hands off her."

Noah drops his hand as heat flares up my neck, then my cheeks. I'm panting when someone switches the bedroom light on, and I have to shield my face from the brightness.

"Who's there?" Noah asks, looking around nervously.

The dork storks.

Silas Huxley, Damon Brooks, and Jude Vanderbilt step out from the ensuite bathroom, but I don't look at them. I keep my eyes on Noah.

Why are they here? Why are they hiding out in the bathroom?

"Oh," Noah breathes, laughing as his posture relaxes.

"Get the fuck out of here, you dorks. This party is for cool people only."

Shame and humiliation flare through me, and I pull my dress down as I walk to the door.

"Where the fuck do you think you're going, Lennon?" Noah asks from behind me.

Why am I embarrassed? I don't care what the dork storks think. I turn around and cross my arms, suddenly feeling brave since there are three other people in this room.

This is my chance to get away from him.

"I'm leaving, Noah."

I don't stay long enough to see if Noah confronts Silas, Damon, or Jude, but by the time I find Mindy dancing with some random junior, I spy Noah in the kitchen throwing back shots. Mindy's dance buddy offers to get us drinks, so we let him, and soon enough, the night begins to pass quickly in a strange, alcohol-induced haze. My hair ends up in a high bun since I'm sweating, and I must ditch my shoes at some point because I don't realize I'm barefoot until my feet hit the cold, stone tiles of the bathroom a couple of hours later.

When I exit, the hallway is empty. I'm about to turn the corner when Damon Brooks walks into me.

"Sorry," he mumbles, looking down at me through his thick, dark lashes.

"Watch where you're going," I reply, annoyance lacing my words.

I make it two feet before Silas is there, with Jude next to him.

"Lennon," Silas mutters.

Something about him, about the kindness on his face, despite the way I treat him, it jolts through me in a single burst of anger.

He feels bad for me.

And what he saw tonight? What he *heard*? Embarrassment floods me all over again.

I shove him backward, baring my teeth as his body hits the opposite wall. He's a little bit taller than me, but I must have at least twenty pounds on him.

"Lennon," he says, his voice more stern this time. "Stop."

I clench my jaw as they circle me. "Stop what? Get out of my way, dorks."

"Did he hurt you?"

I slowly twist around to face Jude.

Jude fucking Vanderbilt. One of the richest boys in our class, and that's saying a lot. He had so much potential, so much of his future ahead of him. But he chose to cling to the geek squad. I cock my head.

"I'm fine. Get out of my way."

I push against Damon this time, and he lets me pass through. I let out an exasperated huff as I try to put distance between myself and the dork storks.

"I see you, Lennon."

Silas's words stop me in my tracks, and I spin around. The kindness I see there, the empathy, cuts right through to the very core of who I am.

Of *what* I am.

And I see myself through his eyes. Digging through

the garbage as a gangly fourteen-year-old. I don't even think he remembers that, but I do. The shame followed me for weeks. *Months.* He sees me pushing back against the teachers. And now? He was a witness to Noah almost assaulting me. In his eyes, I'm a wreck—a *mess*. There is nothing worthy about me, yet when these three guys look at me...

I blink a few times, trying to dispel the tears that begin to prick at the corners of my eyes.

"Lennon?" Noah comes around the corner, glancing between the four of us. "What's going on?"

I *hate* the remorseful looks on Silas, Damon, and Jude's faces. The sorrow, the understanding. White, hot rage fills me. I never want to see that look on anyone's face again. I glance up at Noah, cross my arms, and narrow my eyes at Silas Huxley.

"If you ever touch me again, I will call the cops."

Noah moves before asking questions. He's huge, and he has Silas backed up against the wall in less than a second.

"What the fuck did you do to her, you piece of shit?"

I don't look up at Silas.

I can't.

Instead, I tap my foot on the floor and look down as people come to observe what all the commotion is about. I hadn't noticed earlier, but the music is softer now. Of course everyone heard Noah scream at Silas.

Noah's football friends come around the corner of the hallway, and before I know it, they're dragging the three dork storks away by the collars of their shirts.

Swallowing thickly, I ignore the guilt settling in my belly like a heavy stone. Instead, I find Mindy and tell her that I want to leave.

Even though we're sober now, we decide to catch a cab, and I plug in our address for the ride share company. We wait on the sofa until I get a notification that the driver is outside, and I brace myself for what I'm about to see.

A crowd has gathered in Noah's driveway, and I see three crumpled bodies on the ground. The concrete is red. Someone's bleeding, and there's blood on Noah's hands. My eyes flick to his, and he nods once before kicking Silas again. Biting my lower lip, I look away and walk to the silver car, Mindy chattering beside me about the junior guy she has now claimed as her own. I try to pay attention, nodding and humming at the right times. But my ears are ringing with shame, with guilt. It's going to make me sick.

I can't tear my eyes away from Silas, Damon, and Jude.

I watch them for as long as we can, for as long as the window will allow me to. When I can't anymore, I take a deep breath, close my eyes, and vow never to think of any of them again.

nine

Lennon

Present

I don't want to go to work today. My body is protesting, and even though I slept until noon, I don't feel rested *at all.* Instead, the backs of my thighs ache from scrubbing the floors, and the sides of my arms sting from all the manual labor. I didn't get back to my apartment until nearly four. The guys all sat around and drank beer, not saying a single word to me as I cleaned up their stations. Silas asked me to do inventory at two, and I nearly started crying myself to sleep right then and there.

But I refused to give in.

I refused to acknowledge the grudge they still hold against me from ten years ago, refused to give in to their revenge plot.

They wanted me to scrub the floors? Okay, I'd scrub

those damn floors. Count glove boxes and disinfectant wipe packets until my eyes nearly bled? Sure. It didn't matter to me. I felt like a hollow shell of my former self, anyway. It wasn't like they were going to break me. Not when there was nothing left to break.

I yawn and get up to make some toast as I get ready to meet Mindy for coffee in thirty minutes. Showering quickly, I throw my hair up, step into some leggings, a cropped tank top, and my Birkenstocks. I glance at myself in the mirror, repeating some of the things I was taught in therapy. I grew up without parental mentors, which left me insanely insecure, so I had to do the hard work and relearn how to love myself. Instead of saying I look sloppy, I rephrase it–I don't look sloppy, I look *casual.*

I walk up to the town square and cross the main street, heading into the park. The café we're meeting at is a cute, little pastry shop that sells tea and scones. It's on the other side of the square, and I get there ten minutes early. Grabbing a table outside, I watch the pastry chef inside as she rolls something out in the kitchen. It looks like the start of croissants. One of my favorites. Jealousy flares through me, and I swallow as she makes eye contact with me. I would kill to own a shop like this, to bake all day long, to watch as people eat my creations. In the grand scheme of things, that is my ultimate goal, but I've never had a chance to really go after it.

I'm still daydreaming when Mindy walks up to our table.

"Oh my God," she squeals, grinning as I stand to give her a big hug. "You literally haven't changed at all."

"I could say the same thing about you," I reply, smiling.

She looks exactly the same, except maybe a bit more tired. My eyes widen when she sets a car seat down at her feet.

"When did you have a third baby?" I ask, my eyebrows rising.

She giggles and sits just as the tiny creature begins to stir. "Gabriel wore me down." I smirk, and she leans back in her seat. "What can I say? I love babies."

I laugh and order us both some coffee and a scone—something I decide to splurge on, since Silas *did* hand me nearly two-hundred dollars last night. When I rejected that amount, he just glowered at me and told me to stop asking questions or I was fired.

"I had no idea you were even pregnant."

She grins down at her baby, rocking the car seat with her foot. "Yeah, well, the other two trolls kept me too busy to post anything on social media."

I put my elbows on the table and watch Mindy as she soothes her baby. In high school, Mindy was a party girl—always out, always dating, always had the scoop on where to go. She was outgoing and fun... the complete opposite of me. And her family took me in as one of their own for nearly four years. It's not fair that she looks the same, either. Gorgeous, naturally bronzed skin, deep-set brown eyes, and thick, black hair. I was always envious of her gorgeous hair, which she has up in a casual ponytail today.

"How's Gabriel?" I ask, referring to her husband.

It was kind of a scandal back in the day—Mindy marrying Gabriel. He was ten years older than her, and recently divorced. But here they are, ten years later, with three kids. Despite everything, she's glowing. I can tell she's happy. It's the kind of happy you feel in your soul. The kind I yearn for.

"He's great! Still working too many hours at the firm, but it's fine. I can't complain." She looks at me, *really* looks at me, and I squirm in my seat under her scrutiny.

"Are *you* okay?"

I'd given her a brief summary of what had happened to me this past week, and she'd been understanding and sympathetic. But that familiar, nagging feeling of dread, of someone feeling pity for me, returns full force.

"I'm fine," I say quickly as the server brings our food and drinks. Sipping my coffee, I shrug, trying to think of a way to convince my former best friend that I'm not falling apart at the seams. "I've found a part-time job until I get my feet back on the ground."

Mindy eats her scone in three bites, giving me an apologetic look. "Sorry, I'm ravenous thanks to this one sucking the life force out of me every two hours." Pinning me with a serious stare, she brushes her hands off and tilts her head. "But are you okay, Lennon? You just seem..." She trails off and leans back in her chair. "I'm worried about you. Your eyes are sad, you know?"

I tamp down the irrational anger at her concern.

"Yes. I'm really fine. Wright is..." I swallow. "He's a piece of shit. Honestly? I dodged a bullet."

Mindy laughs. "You really did. Cheating asshole."

I nod. "I'm staying at one of my mom's properties. It's right in town," I add, looking away. "It's small, but it's free. I'll be out of there and into a place of my own in no time."

Mindy orders another scone, setting down a ten-dollar bill in the process. "Oh, yeah. Where is that again?"

I am dreading this question, because I know exactly what she's going to ask next. "It's right over Savage Ink."

She gasps. "Oh my God. Silas's place?!"

I rear my head back. "Yeah. You know it?"

She stands excitedly, pulling her pants down to show off a butterfly tattoo on her lower abdomen.

"I got this to commemorate my C-section." She laughs. "Motherhood is so glamorous."

I chuckle. "Wait, so did he give you that tattoo?"

She shakes her head as she inhales her second scone. "No. Jude Vanderbilt. The two of them own it with Damon Brooks. I'm not complaining, though." She laughs, sipping her coffee. "Like, damn, boys, what the fuck did you eat after high school to get so big? I can't believe how much they've changed."

I burst out laughing and shake my head. "Right? It's almost unnatural."

She smiles at me. "So, what's next, then? Do you plan on staying in Greythorn indefinitely?"

I look down at my chipped nails, and I realize the last time I had them done was in New York.

That's how recently my other life ended.

My *nails* are the same as when I was still engaged to Wright. When I still had a penthouse suite overlooking Central Park, and a housekeeper.

I shake the thought away. "Um, I'm not sure, really. I'd like to get a place of my own here, and after that, I have no idea. Maybe Boston, or maybe somewhere warm like California."

"That's exciting!" Mindy chirps, her voice upbeat. "You have your whole life ahead of you. The world is your oyster."

I nod and chew on my scone. "I guess. I think I'm still in shock."

"Well, do you need a job? I can probably ask Gabriel if he knows of any admin openings—"

"No, it's fine," I interrupt, my stomach doing nervous flip-flops. "I work at Savage Ink part-time."

Mindy's jaw quite literally drops. "Really?" Her eyes scan mine in surprise. "That's..." She clutches her chest and chuckles. "I am shook."

I smirk. "Me too."

"Did they—do they remember *who* you are?!"

Laughing, I shrug. "I mean, Silas told me to go fuck myself when he saw me, so yeah. But I think they were in a pickle and had no other option. Plus, they're totally using the job as a way to get back at me for graduation night."

"Oh my God, I wasn't even referring to graduation night. I forgot about that."

"You *were* quite drunk," I muse, remembering Mindy drooling all over my shoulder on the ride home.

Her smile softens, and she looks down at her baby. "God, how times have changed."

I reach out for her hand. "Thank God they have. I was a bitch in high school."

"I liked you," she whines. "Maybe that makes me a bitch, too."

We both laugh for what feels like an hour, and by the time Lawrence—Mindy's son—wakes up, I'm paying for the check. I say goodbye to them, and we decide to make this a weekly thing. Her two other kids are in school during the day, and damn, it felt really good to see her. I'm still smiling by the time I walk back to my apartment, and even though the death metal begins to play from downstairs half a second after I shut my door, I can't find it in myself to care.

Maybe Mindy was right. Maybe this is going to be my fresh start, and that I need to start thinking about this change as my life beginning—not ending.

ten

Silas

"Fifty bucks says she won't even show up tonight," Damon muses as he plays with his switchblade. "She'll go crying to daddy, he'll pay for a nicer place, and *voila*. We never have to see Lennon Rose again."

"Didn't her dad die recently?" Jude asks, sipping his beer.

I shrug. "Who gives a fuck? The point is, if she comes back tonight, maybe we should—"

"Maybe we should what?" We all twist around at the light, tinkling voice coming from the doorway. "Did you honestly think I wouldn't show up after a few gross chores?" Lennon snorts, setting her purse down behind the desk as she rolls her eyes.

Adrenaline begins to course through me as I stand.

It's always fight or flight with her. I'm on the defensive, even though she's now half my size.

"You're early," I chastise, crossing my arms.

She plops down in the desk chair and leans back. She's chewing on something—candy, from the smell of it—and she just smiles up at me.

I ignore the way that smile sends a jolt to my traitorous dick.

"Yes, well, I wanted to be sure I got the housekeeping done before the customers start to walk in. I was a bit distracted last night between scrubbing shit off the toilet and cleaning scummy trash cans between clients. I know they probably don't appreciate it, either. You know, since Savage Ink prides itself on its customer service, after all."

Speechless.

She's rendered me speechless.

This time, it's Jude who saunters up to her. She stiffens as he walks closer, and I watch the two of them as he stops right in front of her, his hands in his pockets.

"Does it make you sad that your fiancé cheated on you, Lennon?"

Even I flinch at that.

Lennon's face crumples, and her composure disappears. I see the emotions flitting across her pretty little face one by one—shock, confusion, and then... devastation.

She clears her throat. "How do you know about that?"

Jude shrugs. "I heard you were engaged. Now you're

here. I'm not an idiot." He smirks down at her. "Thanks for confirming, though."

Anger. That's solely anger flashing through her attempt at a controlled expression. She takes a deep breath, nostrils flaring, but Damon steps forward.

"I don't give a fuck who is cheating on who. Jude, get back to your station." He looks at me. "You too, Silas." He gives Lennon an unrelenting scowl. "Clean the gum off the side of the building."

Her eyes widen. "Seriously?"

I smile as I walk back to my station. "We don't have the right tools, so you'll have to use your hands." Flicking my eyes to her pink nails, I grin. "I guess it's a good thing you have long nails. I'd use gloves if I were you. That shit is disgusting."

I see it then. The glimmer of doubt. The look of hesitation. Turning around, I wink at the guys.

She thought she had the upper hand, but what she didn't realize was that we are never going to let her have that control over us ever again.

eleven

Lennon

I won't cry.

I won't cry.

I won't cry.

I refuse to *ever* give these pricks the satisfaction of letting them know they got to me. But as I scrape the sticky, years-old gum off the exterior wall, I can't help but want to release a sob as pieces of the disgusting gum press under the tips of my nails, causing them to ache. The gloves did nothing, since they ripped two minutes in. No one talks about the sickly-sweet scent of old gum, either. That smell doesn't just go away—it turns rancid. I gag as I scrape another small section off.

I can leave.

The thought flits through my mind every twenty

seconds or so, with every flurry of motion to get the gum to dislodge from under my nails.

The problem is, if I walked away now, they would always hold that against me. I would always be the loser in their eyes.

Grinding my jaw, I continue until an idea strikes me. I walk around the corner, heading up into my apartment, and grab the only thing that makes sense—a pie server. I take a butter knife down with me, too.

I head back inside the studio twenty minutes later, smiling, the pie server and knife safely back in my apartment, where I'll probably end up recycling them thanks to that God-awful smell. Silas just raises his eyebrows before going out to check my work.

Prick.

I pretend to be busy on the computer for the next half hour or so, and I thank my lucky stars that the first customer is a few minutes early. The night passes similarly, and maybe the guys got their fill of revenge already, because they don't ask me to do any more ridiculous chores. Around two, I tell them I'm leaving, and they all wave me away. I'm both surprised and worried at that. Surprised they're just going to let me go, and worried they're gearing up for something bigger. Tomorrow is my day off, and Mindy is going to come over for some wine, so at least I can put off whatever they have in store for me until Saturday.

Just as I open the door to leave, Silas walks over to me with yet another wad of cash.

I quickly count it. "This is three hundred dollars."

He shrugs. "We pay $20/hour."

I glare at him, doing the math. "I wasn't here for fifteen hours."

He sits down on the couch, and my eyes flick over to Damon and Jude, who are both watching me with large frowns. My eyes go back to Silas as he runs a hand through his messy, blonde hair.

"Do you want the fucking money or not? Overtime is double, and you worked overtime both nights. Take the money and get the fuck out of here, Lennon."

I swallow, pocketing the cash. "Okay. See you Saturday."

Like always, neither of them acknowledges me, and I slink upstairs to my apartment. As I close the door, I can hear them laughing downstairs, and my chest tightens. I shake my head and take a long, hot shower before climbing into bed for the night.

I'm so tired that I'm not even hungry, but the day's events keep replaying in my head, so I grab my phone out of instinct. My thumb hovers over Wright's contact, and I have to force myself *not* to text him. What would I say, anyway? There's nothing left between us, no unfinished business other than closure on my part. Instead, I open Instagram for the first time since I left New York, and my feed is full of Wright and his friends—and *her*.

I grind my teeth as I sit up in bed and stare at the pretty, petite redhead in Wright's arms at a bonfire last night. Clicking over to her profile, I see she has a picture of herself at the penthouse from a few days ago. My throat constricts as I realize the duvet she has wrapped around her is the one I bought Wright for Christmas, and when I look closer, I can see that she's wearing the robe he bought *me* three years ago on Valentine's Day. I'd left it all there—anything and everything that reminded me of him, aside from the bare necessities. But now, as I hug my knees to my chest and my lower lip wobbles... I can't help but think that maybe I made a mistake.

Those are *my* things, too.

I had a life there, full of pots and pans that I carefully selected, and dish towels that I commissioned from a local linen vendor. The art, the curtains, the giant twelve-pound candle that I painstakingly made one winter out of boredom...

Those are *my* things. And Wright gave them away to the next girl.

I erased an entire ten years of my life, and now I have no idea where or how I'm supposed to start over.

Tears spring loose from the corners of my eyes, and my body shakes with sobs as I hug my knees tighter. This wasn't how my life was supposed to end up—alone, in a studio apartment, working for three guys who would rather see me dead than alive. I cry harder, louder, letting every emotion escape until I'm practically wailing. I promise myself that I will go back soon for the things that mean the most—the candle, the artwork, my baking supplies, and anything that's irreplaceable. I still have a key.

Wiping my cheeks, I get up and grab a tissue, then crawl back under the covers. I close my eyes, shivering, and fall asleep with my arms wrapped around myself.

twelve

Lennon

"Oh my God," Mindy croons, sipping her wine on my couch. "I haven't had a proper night away from the kids in years." She laughs before hiccupping. "Not to say that Gabriel isn't great—he is. But I'll be honest and say that I just don't have a lot of friends," she says bluntly, and we both laugh.

"I *had* a lot of friends, but none of them were actually friends, you know?"

I lean back on my sofa as Mindy nods. She'd gotten here about an hour ago, breast pump in tow, and she is now two glasses into the nice bottle of Sauvignon Blanc I bought with Silas's money. My stomach flips when I think about that. About him, and the way he, Damon, and Jude all seem to hate me—but not enough that I have to worry about money. It's confusing, infuriating, and overwhelming.

"Honestly, I think that's worse," she muses, finishing her glass. "You think they have your back, and then they don't. Ugh." She looks at me and smiles. "At least I know I'm a loner and can prepare for it."

I laugh. "Agreed. I'd much rather be a loner."

Mindy smiles and rests her head against the back of the couch. Even as a mom of three, she's wearing jeans, heels, and a green silk blouse that makes her golden skin glow. I, on the other hand, am wearing baggy mom jeans and an old band t-shirt. I stand and walk over to the kitchen, pouring us both the last of the bottle.

"You've changed," Mindy says softly.

I sit back down and hand her glass over to her as I cock my head. "How so?"

She shrugs. "I don't know. You're a lot less... jaded."

I raise my eyebrows and look down. "Jaded?"

She leans forward. "Well, yeah. I mean... I know high school was rough for you. And forgive me for saying this, but I think you acted out against... you know."

My parents.

My neglect.

I pull my lower lip between my teeth as I ruminate on her words. She's not wrong, but I guess I'm surprised she was able to deduce what was happening. Maybe I shouldn't be. Maybe it was totally obvious to anyone paying attention, and I just ignored it. She's a bright, astute person. It's no wonder she figured out my situation, even when I tried my very hardest to ignore and deflect.

"Lots of therapy," I joke, giving her a small smile.

She reaches over and grabs the hand I have resting on the back of the couch. "Me too. For different reasons." She pauses as her eyes rove over my face. "I hope you know that I'm proud of who you've become."

I squeeze her hand. "A twenty-eight-year-old who lives in a studio apartment that her mom owns?"

She pulls her lips to one side. "You know what I mean, smartass. Starting over. Taking a risk. Leaving your douche canoe of a fiancé."

I laugh. "He is such a douche canoe."

"Seriously, though. I know your life is chaotic and crazy right now, but you seem to have come into yourself these last ten years. And I want you to know that you can always count on me as a friend." She smiles. "A *real* friend."

I swallow thickly, tamping down the emotion that begins to ache in my chest. I always do this. I always reject real feelings. I push them away in favor of humor and ignorance. Nobody modeled love for me while I was growing up, so I'm still unsure of how to process it when it happens. So, I squeeze Mindy's hand again in a silent thank you.

"I have another bottle of wine, and then I thought we could watch a movie?" I suggest.

Mindy scoffs, letting go of my hand as she shakes her head. "This is my one night away from the kids. How about I pump while we finish that bottle, and then we go out?"

I look down at myself, wholly unprepared to go out into the real world with other people.

"Out? Where?"

She shrugs as she pulls her blouse off, exposing a nursing bra. "There are a few bars here, or we could get a cab and head into Boston."

"I don't even think I own real shoes," I say slowly. "I left in such a rush..."

Mindy stops assembling her pump and gives me a large smile. "Let me help you. Just show me what I'm working with, and I'll find something for you."

That feeling comes back. The heavy, intense warmth that makes me so uncomfortable, and makes me feel hugely undeserving. I shift in my seat and sigh.

"Sure. Okay."

She grins, showing off her white teeth and megawatt smile. "Good." Hooking herself up, she leans back. "Let me just milk myself and then we can go."

I laugh and grab the second bottle, wondering all the while what it would've been like to have had Mindy in my life these last ten years.

Mindy manages to make me look half presentable, letting me borrow her blouse and heels as she steals one of my crop tops and boots. It all works together, and by the time we walk out of my apartment, we're stumbling and trying not to fall as we make our way down the narrow staircase. *Were heels always this treacherous, or did I just drink too much? It's been a few years since I've worn them since Wright was always insecure about his height...*

We walk past Savage Ink, and the guys are busy with clients in the back. Lola is chatting to a client up front. She doesn't see us, and I drag Mindy away before that changes. The last thing I need is for Silas, Damon, and Jude to see me drunk. We walk down the main street until we get to The Queen's Arms, a small pub that's always busy. I've never been here, though I remember it from my childhood.

I grab us a table while Mindy buys us drinks, and I look around as I get settled. A few familiar faces look back at me, so I pretend to be texting on my phone even though I have no one to text. God forbid someone comes up to me and wants to talk...

"Alright, so apparently gin and tonics are their specialty. Hope you like gin." She cackles, setting down two enormous goblets full of ice and clear liquid. "That's all gin, by the way." She pulls two small, glass bottles out of her back pockets. "We add the tonic ourselves."

I eye the goblet warily, but we add our tonic and gulp our drinks down in no time. I catch her up on what it's like working at Savage Ink, and she tells me all about life as a mom of three. It makes me a tiny bit excited for the future, albeit a little sad that I don't have anyone in mind to share it all with. I once thought it would be Wright, but he was never sold on the idea of kids. I wanted them and thought after we got married that I could change his mind.

For the first time since everything happened, relief washes over me.

Maybe everything *did* happen for a reason.

That thought causes me to buy our next round of giant gin and tonics, and by the time we finish those, the pub is packed full of people and the music begins to play.

"Oh my God, I love this song!" Mindy squeals, grabbing my hand and dragging me out onto the dance floor.

"I don't dance!" I scream over the music.

"You do tonight!" she yells back. "Come on."

The music gets louder, and people begin to sing along. I can't help but grin and close my eyes, taking in the noise, the voices, and the general feeling of belonging. Another song comes on—one that I actually know the words to—and Mindy and I scream the lyrics as we jump up and down to the beat. I feel strong arms behind me, and when I turn around, a handsome, older gentleman is smiling down at me, asking me to dance. Mindy wiggles her eyebrows at me, and I let him lead me to the edge of the dance floor as a slower song comes on.

Keeping an eye on Mindy, we sway to the music, and I inhale his unfamiliar scent. It's nice—vetiver and something else that smells like pine trees. He's tall, clean-shaven, with black and gray hair and a chiseled jaw.

"Do you live in Greythorn?" the man asks, his voice low and husky.

I nod. "Yep. Just moved back after ten years away."

His brown eyes light up. "Wow. What brought you back?"

I shrug. "Life."

He lifts a hand and runs it down my jaw, and for a second, a single second, I contemplate what it would be like to bring this guy home. I am not beholden to anyone, and once Mindy goes back to her house...

Speaking of, I crane my neck around and scan the crowd for my friend, but I don't see her.

"I'm sorry. I need to find my friend. She's really drunk."

He nods. "Nice meeting you..." He widens his eyes, waiting for me to tell him my name.

"Lennon," I say, a genuine smile on my face. He's nice, and he has kind eyes. A bit older than me, but who cares? He's cute, and presumably single, since there's no ring on his left finger.

"And where can I find you, Lennon?" he asks, his smile mischievous.

"I work at the front desk of Savage Ink."

Shut up, Lennon. What are you doing?

The smile drops from his face. "Savage Ink?"

I take a step back. "Yes?"

He shakes his head and rubs his lip with his thumb. "Excuse my language, but what the *fuck* are you doing working for those guys?"

I swallow, my eyes widening. "What do you mean?"

"Listen, Lennon. You need to be careful. Those guys are unhinged," he states gruffly.

Shivers work their way down my spine. "Unhinged? How so?"

He gives me a grim smile. "You don't want to know, baby girl."

His use of *baby girl* makes me uncomfortable.

"Thanks. I appreciate the warning."

"Anytime. Hope to see you around." He winks, and then he walks off.

I spin around and find Mindy slumped against one of the booths. I rush over, and when I shake her, she snorts and sits up.

"It's your turn to get up with him," she slurs, without even opening her eyes, before resting her cheek on her arms as she leans forward on the table.

"Come on, Mind. Let's get you home," I say gently, and then I lift her up and walk her out of the pub.

I call a cab and give them her address, and she gives me a quick hug before hopping in the back with her bag—which includes her pump, bless her.

"Hey, if you ever need me to come over and watch the kids while you nap, let me know."

"You're the best, Len," she says, blowing me a kiss. "See you soon."

I wave her off, sighing as I begin my walk back to my apartment. I'm still completely drunk, and since it's nearly two in the morning, the main street is empty. A layer of fog clings to the streetlamps, and I shiver as the wind picks up. *God, it's eerie here at night.*

I'm about a block away from home when I hear footsteps behind me. I look over my shoulder as I quicken my pace, and I don't see anything out of the ordinary. Walking faster, I'm five doors down from Savage Ink, near the back alley where the communal dumpster is located, when a rough hand grabs me.

thirteen

Damon

I wrap my arms around Lennon tightly as Jude beckons us over to the back door of Savage. She screams and thrashes against me, and even though she's a tall girl, she doesn't have any muscle on her. I grit my jaw at the thought of her not being able to fight back against someone else—someone *worse*.

"What the *fuck* are you guys doing?" she asks roughly through jagged breaths, baring her teeth at all of us. The buttons pucker on her blouse, and I have to tear my eyes away from her tits straining against the silky material as we move.

"Righting a wrong," Silas growls, moving us inside the studio. After he closes the door, we all release her, and she stumbles forward, grabbing onto the desk before whirling around and facing us with a furious expression.

I must admit, she's kind of cute when she's angry.

"You're all fucking psychos," she snarls, grabbing her purse from where Jude threw it on the ground. Walking toward the door, she stiffens when she sees who's slumped over the chair by the door.

"It's locked," I muse, smiling. "Oh, and as you can see, we have a guest."

Lennon's fists open and close at her sides as she studies the man in the chair, and then she twists around.

"Is this some kind of sick joke?" She nudges the man with her toes. "How did you—"

"Homeboy came in for a tattoo," Jude responds leisurely, picking at a thread on his shirt. "I took the opportunity upon myself to... *enhance* the beer we offered him."

She scoffs. "You fucking roofied Noah Adelmann?!" She turns to face all of us. "Why?"

Silas steps forward. "This isn't a favor to you, princess. But we thought you'd want to see the other side of Savage Ink. Maybe this will be enough to make you reconsider working for us."

Her face goes white, and I almost have to laugh at how terrified she looks. I take a step toward her, holding out my butterfly knife. Her gaze flits from the knife and back to my eyes, and then she looks over at Noah as she pieces the situation together.

"You—you're going to *kill* him?"

I grin. "No, princess. *You* are."

fourteen

Lennon

The man's warning from earlier clangs through my mind.

You need to be careful. Those guys are unhinged.

Unhinged.

I flick my eyes between the three of them, palms sweating. My chest rises and falls quickly because of the exertion of trying to fight them off, and I look over at Noah.

Noah freaking Adelmann.

I hadn't seen him since that graduation party. Not since he beat the shit out of Silas, Damon, and Jude. If anything, this is *their* retribution. Not mine. I'd moved on and tried to forget about that night. Whenever I did think of it, an inky mass of guilt would lodge in my belly, so I just ignored it altogether—the thing with Noah, and then what happened afterward.

But was it bad enough to kill him?

I scour my memory of that night, going over every little detail. I'd left early, and I hadn't seen the outcome of the fight, nor did I want to know. I kept my head down all summer, secluding myself at Mindy's house and making an excuse for leaving for Cambridge two weeks early. I needed to get out of Greythorn. I couldn't wait to leave.

But this was not worth murdering Noah for. That night... nothing happened to me that night.

Thanks to the three of them...

I look up at Damon Brooks. "You can't be serious?"

Damon walks closer, the creaking of the wood floor getting louder the closer he gets. He gives me a monstrous smile, the kind of smile that has ice seeping into my bones.

"I spent two weeks in the hospital for a broken rib. It punctured my lung." I wince. He continues. "Three of Silas's teeth are veneers, and he had to save up for them, since his parents refused to pay." My eyes find Silas's over Damon's shoulder, and he glares right back at me. My heart leaps into my throat. "And Jude? He pissed himself. The psychological toll—"

"Damon."

Jude's commanding voice causes me to scan his face, the beautiful yet deadly face. And I realize, with a sinking, dreadful feeling, that I might be in over my head with these guys. That my life after high school was *so* much different than theirs.

Ten years can make a person, or it can breed a monster.

In my case, three monsters.

A cold sweat breaks out all over my skin, and the back of my neck begins to tingle as I realize where I am, and who I'm with—and the fact that they seem hellbent on retribution. Clearly, they've done this before.

Noah was an ass to them, sure, but I was worse.

I was the snake in their lives, miserable and always waiting to strike. Noah may have kicked their asses, but every day I attempted to break their souls.

I wish I could say I didn't know any better, but I knew what I was doing. I was scared and insecure, and it took a solid five years of therapy to come to terms with that. I wanted to reach out to them over the years, but I also didn't want to reopen any wounds. In my eyes, we'd all moved on—me, especially. I was no longer a bully, no longer feeding off people who saw the real me, no longer tearing people down just to make myself feel better. I did the work. I spent many sleepless nights wishing I'd been better, wishing I could apologize. Not just to them, but to everyone.

But as Noah stirs before me, and Damon continues holding the knife out to me, I realize that while I was paying a fortune for Eye Movement Desensitization and Reprocessing therapy, journaling, *healing*... Silas, Damon, and Jude were stewing in their anger.

And this is the result.

I look up at Damon and cross my arms. "I'm not going to kill Noah Adelmann."

"Go on, princess," Jude says, his voice like velvet. "We know you want to."

I shake my head, swallowing the bile that's beginning to rise in my throat. "Why would I want to kill him?"

Silas takes a step forward, his icy blue eyes pinning me to the spot. "Because we saw what happened."

He sounds angry. Like, really, *really* angry.

"Nothing happened—"

"Are you in denial, or do you actually not remember this motherfucker grooming you for a year and then attempting to rape you?"

At Jude's words, the blood in my veins turns to ice.

Realization slams into me. He's right—I *am* in denial. I have been since that night. Whenever my therapist asked about it, I would always lie and say I got too drunk and went home sick. Because I did. I vomited my guts up that night.

But not because I was too drunk.

And then I think of Noah Adelmann. A twenty-two-year-old who befriended a sixteen-year-old. Who used to pick her up in his Mustang and take her for ice cream. Who would talk shit about Mindy and try to isolate me from my friends. Who would text me inappropriate things that I thought were *normal* at the time, because I was vulnerable. Because I didn't know better, and I didn't have anyone looking out for me. And that night, if Silas, Damon, and Jude hadn't been there...

If it would make you feel better, we can keep this a secret. Just between you and me.

I take a few steadying breaths and look over at Noah. He's older, obviously, but he looks... sad. He has a weathered face and a beer gut now, and a bald patch on the top of his head. I do the math and realize he's thirty-two. There's a wedding ring around his swollen ring finger, and even though the hatred that runs through me is potent, I also feel bad for him. Still living in Greythorn, looking old and exhausted...

"What did he come in for?" I ask, and I can see Damon's eyes widen in surprise as he plays with his knife. "The tattoo. What did he ask for?"

"His daughter's initials. She's two, apparently." I swallow. A daughter. A *baby*. He's someone's *father*. I open my mouth to ask him to let Noah go when Damon interrupts me. "He tore up his knee playing college football, so he ended up becoming the girls' volleyball coach at Ravenwood Academy. There are... rumors... that he acts inappropriately with some of them. Last year, he almost got fired for sleeping in one of their rooms during an away game."

I look between the three of them. "He *wasn't* fired for that?"

Silas shrugs, coming to stop right in front of me. "You remember who his father is, right?"

My heart races. Carlisle Adelmann. Superintendent of Greythorn School District. I'd completely forgotten that fact—how Noah seemed to get away with anything.

Including hanging out with high school girls at

twenty-two...

Damon and Jude come to stand next to Silas. Confusion muddles my brain, and I'm unable to move, to speak. Yes, they had ten years to stew in their anger, but maybe it didn't corrode their souls.

Maybe it just fueled the fire.

I look at each of them. At Damon's rough demeanor, at Jude's deadly stillness, at Silas's tortured soul—and suddenly, I'm not scared anymore.

They didn't turn into monsters.

They just began hunting them.

"Killing him would feel good," Jude muses, taking Damon's knife from his hand. "But we're not going to kill him tonight, princess."

My head spins. "But I thought—"

"He's not worth the jail time," Silas clarifies, his arms crossed as he narrows his eyes at Noah.

I nod to the knife in Jude's hands. "What's that for?"

Damon grins as he cracks his neck and takes the knife from Jude. "A few days ago, I spoke to the girl on his team. The one he slept in the same room with. She's graduating this year, and refuses to press charges, but she admitted that he raped her. She said no, and he did it anyway," he growls. "She's seventeen." He looks at me. "Just like you were."

My stomach churns. "Jesus."

He hands the knife to me. "If you want to hurt him, we won't judge you."

I take the knife—the porcelain handle and the shiny, sharp steel—and I look over at Noah. The knife clatters to the ground, and I shake my head, turning to face them again.

"No. I don't want to hurt him."

Silas smirks. "Good girl."

Jude walks over to me and looks down at me with a scowl. "You passed the test. Welcome to the dark side of Savage Ink, Lennon. Sit down," he commands, pointing to the chair across from Noah.

"Wait," I say, my voice a little louder than before. "What the fuck do you mean, I passed the test?"

"Sit down, Lennon," Damon growls. His voice is menacing, and I see him pick the knife up before he quirks his eyebrows in my direction.

I walk over and sit, my legs still shaking, and a flurry of motion happens as Silas injects Noah with something else and they all lower him to the ground. And then...

"Oh my God," I whisper, watching as Silas cleans his forehead with an antibacterial wipe for thirty seconds. I point to the wipe. "Does that really matter in the grand scheme of things?"

He's going to tattoo Noah's forehead.

Tattoo. His. Forehead.

"If it gets infected," Silas starts, continuing to wipe in large circles, "the writing might get all fucked up."

I laugh and look away. "This is sadistic, you know that, right?"

Jude looks at me and frowns. "He's a rapist, Lennon. You tell me who the sadist is."

Goosebumps erupt along my skin as I watch Silas, Damon, and Jude lift Noah onto one of the leather seats, reclining it fully. Silas snaps plastic gloves onto his hands, and then he looks up at me.

"So? What shall we do?"

I open and close my mouth. "You're asking me?"

He shrugs. "As one of his victims, I thought maybe you'd want a say."

I walk over and look down at Noah. "Do you guys do this a lot?"

I see the three of them share a look. Jude shrugs. "We were known in Boston. Not so much here, though there are people who suspect we get up to no good."

I think of the man in the bar but decide against saying anything. I have a feeling secrets run deeper in Greythorn than I previously thought.

"Rapist," I say quietly. "He raped a girl. He almost raped me. There are probably many others. Now he can't hide from anyone... not even his father."

Silas's eyes find mine, pinning me to my spot. My stomach flutters as his eyes soften just a bit, and something white-hot jolts through me as he winks.

I swallow at the feeling, and he turns his tattoo gun on. The buzzing sound has quickly become a comfortable second nature to me.

"I should pierce his mouth shut," Jude remarks, arms crossed as he leans against his chair and watches Silas. My blood chills at his words.

Silas begins to ink Noah, and the flutters in my stomach grow stronger. My eyes glide over Silas's bare arm, the muscles contracting with every stroke of the tattoo gun, the veins cording his golden skin, running down to his large hand. Swallowing, I clench my thighs together as my heart races in my chest.

I feel someone behind me, but I don't turn around. "What are you thinking, princess?" Jude asks, his breath on my neck. He reaches around and moves my hair over one shoulder. I ignore the way my body trembles ever so slightly in his presence.

"About what you all think of me... how you've treated me until tonight," I murmur, my eyes not leaving Silas and Noah. "What changed?"

"Seeing him," Damon growls, baring his teeth in the direction of Noah's unconscious body. "Remembering that night."

That night.

I suppose I need to get a tattoo one day, too. What would mine say?

Bully.

The word flares through me and nearly knocks me over.

I was a bully. To them, to all three of them, and to some of the other students. I shake my head.

"Will he remember that he came in here tomorrow? How will you cover your tracks?"

Silas chuckles, a deep, low sound as the tattoo gun forms the 'P' on Noah's forehead. He wipes the extra ink away and continues.

"When he wakes up, his forehead will be sore, but he won't remember tonight at all. He was already drunk when he came in, and then we gave him the sedative... he'll be lucky if he remembers his own name."

"It'll be an epic hangover," Damon adds gruffly.

"Don't you have cameras?" I ask, looking around.

Silas shakes his head. "Not tonight, we don't." He swipes the tissue across Noah's forehead again and looks up at me. "There won't be any evidence this ever happened. Aside from his new tattoo."

I wrap my arms around myself, nauseous with the thought of tattooing one word on myself—one fatal flaw. Would they make me do it, eventually? Would they kidnap me and ink me against my will for what I did to them all those years ago? In a way, they were already getting revenge by having me do so many of the tedious chores. Was there more to come–something worse–in my future?

I rub my sweaty palms on my pants, and then I grab my purse from where it lays on the floor.

"I should go," I say quickly, twisting around.

"Lennon," Silas barks, and I still.

"Yeah?" I ask, not daring to turn around, not daring to confirm the pitying expressions on their faces. The anger, the thirst for revenge.

"See you tomorrow," he says after a few seconds.

I wonder what he was about to say. If we were perhaps thinking the same thing.

I walk out the door and turn right, each step up to my apartment slow and heavy because of the alcohol, and the adrenaline that has now given way to utter exhaustion.

I barely make it to my bed before I collapse onto it and fall asleep instantly.

fifteen

Lennon

I wake up thirty minutes before I'm supposed to meet my mom at Café du Pont for lunch. It's a new place, inspired by Parisienne brasseries, and it looks pretty fancy. It wouldn't be Genevieve Rose without a fancy lunch, though, so I'm not surprised. I make a quick cup of coffee and take a few ibuprofens to numb the pounding headache behind my eyes. I shoot a response to Mindy, who had texted me that she'd gotten home in one piece, and then I throw on my most sophisticated dress—which just so happens to be the dress I wore to my engagement party.

Smoothing it down, I look at my reflection.

This isn't me. The white lace, the A-line cut, the neutral sandals, the pearl headband.

I quickly unzip the dress and pull on a form-fitting black maxi dress instead, shaking my hair out and teasing it a bit.

There we go.

Smiling, I exit my apartment and glance into Savage Ink as I walk down the main street. It's empty, of course, but my skin pebbles when I think of what happened to Noah. I wonder if he's awake yet—if he's freaking out. My smile grows slightly, and there's an extra kick in my step, knowing he's suffering, even just a little bit. I'm sure he'll have the tattoo removed, but not before the people closest to him see him for what he is.

Once I arrive, the hostess takes me to the back of the restaurant, which overlooks the central park. There is china laid out at each place setting, along with white linen napkins. I look around for my mother, but I don't see her anywhere. A glance at my watch confirms that she's twelve minutes late. I order us some white wine since I know she loves chardonnay, and then I sit back and wait.

So similar to my childhood—always waiting. Always needing. Always wanting.

I haven't seen my mom since my father's funeral. Wright invited her to the engagement party last year. He even bought her a plane ticket. But she was a no show, and later explained that she hated flying. It hurt, that kind of rejection. It always did, and it never seemed to lessen, even though I was a grown ass woman now. But certain things, like a mother's love, just can't really be found elsewhere. And when it's missing from your life, it feels like a giant void in your chest.

I always think I've gotten used to it, come to terms with it, then something else happens. That wound opens afresh, cutting deep like it always does, bleeding everywhere.

That was life with my mom... one big, gaping wound that never really healed, and hurt extra bad every time it reopened.

I take a few large sips of wine after the server brings our glasses over, and I try to quell the anger that's beginning to rise inside of me at the thought of being stood up by my own mother.

Maybe I should've confirmed today. Maybe she forgot.

I shake my head and close my eyes.

No.

This is exactly the situation my therapist would describe as *not my problem.*

My mother and I confirmed it last night. She's an adult. We had a solid plan to meet at noon. This is all on her. I finish my glass and move onto hers as the time slowly ticks by. I order a plate of fries, and at the hour mark, I pay the bill and leave.

Tears sting the corners of my eyes, but I sweep them away quickly as I stalk to my apartment and turn my phone off. I can't shake the ache in my chest, or the downright *hurt* clawing through me, but I can ensure her inevitable excuses I'm about to hear won't make me feel worse right now. Pulling my dress over my head, I crawl

into bed and let myself sob—hard, unrelenting sobs that shake the bed frame. My body feels bone dry when I finish half an hour later, my eyes nearly swollen shut. I walk to the sink and drink two large glasses of water, and then I proceed to climb back into bed and fall asleep again.

A few hours later, my alarm goes off, alerting me to get ready for work. I take my time in the shower, and then I lie back in bed with cold chamomile tea bags on my eyes to help with the puffiness. They're better now, but they're still a little red and swollen. I let out an exasperated cry when not even concealer can hide my sad eyes, and after another minute of trying, I give up and throw on a black blouse and cut-off shorts, finishing the look with black booties. The guys hopefully won't notice, and if they do, I can at least blame my hangover.

I walk into Savage Ink just a moment later, getting right to work and ignoring the way Silas, Damon, and Jude immediately stop talking as I sit down at the front desk. Opening our email program, I click through and delete all the junk mail, and as I open the first inquiry about a booking, I feel the three guys right in front of me. Then I see them stop in my periphery.

"What?" I ask, my voice caustic.

"What happened to you?" Silas asks, his voice firm and still as death.

I swallow, but I still haven't looked away from the screen as I copy and paste our generic yet personable message about using the online booking system or calling to book an appointment. It was something I did right when I started, something Lola had been typing out each and every time. But this saves me time.

More time for scrubbing toilets, I guess.

"Nothing happened to me. This is how I look when I'm hungover," I reply simply, slamming my finger a little too hard on the delete key.

"Bullshit." Damon's voice is... —angry?

I snap my head up and look at them. "Why do you care? It's evident you all hate me. If the bathroom wasn't enough indication, cleaning the gum off that wall was a crystal-clear message." Silas opens his mouth to reply, but a new wave of frustration hits me, and I stand up from my chair. "Overpaying me because you *pity* me is not being nice. You do it because you feel guilty."

Without another word, I stomp to the bathroom and close the door, my chest rising and falling a few times before I get my breathing under control. *Inhale, exhale.* I use the toilet, wash my hands, and then I stare at my reflection for a minute.

I used to think I was pretty. Large round hazel eyes, long blonde hair, plump lips, long legs... but lately, I don't feel like myself. I still look the same as I did, but the last couple of weeks have taken their toll. My face is weary. Exhausted. I wipe my nose with a tissue and return to the studio. Silas, Damon, and Jude are all prepping their stations now, and none of them look at me this time as I take a seat up front.

The beginning of the night goes smoothly, and I spend a good amount of time responding to their Instagram messages. Lola has been great about posting, but not so great about responding to the 514 messages in their message requests. Around eight, a familiar voice near the front door causes me to tense up and close my eyes.

Please don't let it be her, please don't let it be her—

"Lennon Marie Rose," my mom scoffs, clutching her purse as she wanders into Savage Ink.

Seeing my mom, with her blonde hair, blue eyes, tailored Diane von Furstenberg wrap dress, and a Tiffany necklace, standing in the middle of Savage Ink... is quite hilarious. She stands out like a sore thumb, especially next to Silas's very-tattooed next client. Her hand moves up to her throat as she walks over to me.

"What in tarnation are you doing in here?"

I look around. All three guys are watching me, watching *her*.

"I work here, mom."

Her eyebrows shoot up. "Like hell you do." She looks at Silas. "I hope you're packing your things, Mr. Huxley. Your time in my building is coming to an end."

"What?" I screech, crossing my arms. I spin around to face Silas, Damon, and Jude. Their clients look uncomfortable, so I sigh and turn back to my mom. "Let's go outside."

I don't give her a chance to decline as I loop my arm

through hers and drag her out the door and down the sidewalk.

"Please tell me you're joking," she admonishes as we go three doors down and out of earshot of anyone at Savage. "Your father rented this place to those *heathens.* I have been trying to get them evicted for *two years,*" she seethes. "My word. If I had known—"

"What? Why?"

"This is a respectable community. And those devil worshippers have people come in from all over the country. These people are *riff raff,* Lennon."

"They're nice guys," I say quickly, crossing my arms. "And I needed a job. Because my fiancé cheated on me, and took all of my money. In case you forgot," I add.

She narrows her eyes and puts her hands on her hips. "You don't need to work, honey. How much money do you need?"

I look away and rub the back of my neck. Nothing has changed. Smooth over the mess with things, with money, with material objects. There is no maternal love inside my mother. She doesn't care that my life is a mess. Just like when I was a child. She'd starve me, and then she'd make up for it with a week's worth of Happy Meals. All I wanted was stability, and love. All she ever gave me were excuses.

"I don't need your money," I respond, making sure to articulate each word. "You missed our lunch today."

She scoffs. "I told Fran to email you. I had something come up."

I bite my tongue. I hadn't thought to check my email,

seeing as I've never thought of our rare time together as business transactions. But I guess that only makes one of us.

"You weren't picking up your phone, so I came here to see if you were inside the apartment, and you weren't. But when I walked by and saw you inside that *place*—"

"It's a tattoo studio," I clarify. "They're really talented artists, mom."

She makes a face. "Talented artists? Van Gogh was a talented artist. These guys are—"

"Stop, Mom," I interrupt, my lower lip wobbling. "I *like* working here. My whole life was upended less than two weeks ago, and this place gives me some semblance of stability." I take a deep breath. "I didn't exactly have the warmest of homecomings, either," I say snidely. "What were my options? The house is being renovated, and while I'm grateful for the apartment, it feels like a vacation rental more than anything—"

"You were always so spoiled, do you know that?" my mom says with disdain, and her words snap through me painfully, one at a time.

"Spoiled?" I yell, tears stinging my eyes. "I had to eat out of the garbage cans! Thank God I had friends who took care of me when they could. You and dad would leave for these luxurious trips, and I'd have to fend for myself! It's like you had a kid and decided one day that you didn't want to be parents anymore."

Her lips thin as she looks around. We've amassed a small gathering of people who are watching us fight with feigned concern.

"You were old enough to know how to cook by the time we left you alone," she replies, not even looking at me as she picks at one of her acrylic nails.

As if that's an excuse.

I let out a muffled sob, swiping at my eyes to catch the tears before they trail down my cheeks. "I'm done. This—*you*—coming back here was a mistake."

One thing. I just want one thing from her.

Love.

I turn around, the pain and disappointment swirling in my stomach. It hurts. It always hurts so damn much to see how much she doesn't care about me.

"And where will you go, Lennon?" she asks, her voice cold-hearted and filled with amusement.

My chest heaves as my breath hitches, trying to keep my composure. My mind is jumbled with insults, but I can't seem to utter any of them. My body feels fragmented, like it's breaking, especially my heart. I lower my chin and look at the ground. She's right. I have nowhere else to go. I never did have very many friends. My life revolved around Wright and his friends, who all took his side–even after *he* cheated.

Besides Mindy, I have... no one.

Panic rises in my throat when I realize I'm stuck. Either stuck here, or somewhere else, but either way, I am alone.

Utterly, and completely alone.

"That's what I thought," my mom taunts, straightening and brushing the invisible lint off of her dress. "Now stop acting like a fool. Go back to your apartment, take a shower," she adds, sniffing, "and pack your things. I'll put you up at the Four Seasons—"

"No," I say quietly. "I'm done. I'm twenty-eight years old. Just tell me how much the rent is for the apartment, and I'll pay you for–"

"Are you on drugs, Lennon? I told you, we're going to the Four Seasons."

She reaches out and grabs ahold of my hand, squeezing me firmly and dragging me back toward Savage Ink, and I close my eyes as she leads me away, my tears finally springing free.

"Get your fucking hands off her."

Silas.

She stops suddenly, and I snap my eyes open.

Silas, Damon, and Jude are all staring at my mom with the most menacing of expressions. Jude especially– he looks like he's about to burst a blood vessel in his forehead. If he had a superpower, it would be death by glare. Damon's fists are clenched at his sides, and Silas is breathing heavily. His eyes flick between my mom and me.

"I beg your pardon?" my mom asks, recoiling slightly.

"You heard me," Silas grits out, spitting at her feet.

She shrieks, backing up a step and dropping my hand. "You disgusting, filthy, piece of–"

"I dare you to finish that sentence," Jude says, staring her down.

Something about his voice, the quiet, eerie calm, sends shivers down my spine.

My mom looks at me. "Come on, Lennon. Let's go."

I cross my arms and look between them, the divide between all of us larger now. The people who gathered around my mom and I earlier are still watching, but this time, a few of the people have paler faces now that Silas, Damon, and Jude are here. Go with my mom, or with the guys? One is neglectful, cruel, and bitter. The others are rude, vicious, and brutal. Truth be told, I should probably just walk away from all of them, but I begin to see a precipice opening before me.

Will I choose my own mother, who represents my horrific past?

Or will I choose Savage Ink, which doesn't exactly feel like a better option?

"Go back to the Four Seasons, mom. I'm fine here. I don't want to go with you."

And I don't exactly want to stay, but what choice do I have?

Her face reddens as she opens her mouth for what I'm sure will be a cruel retort.

"Choose your next words wisely," Silas says before she can think to respond, and then he's holding a... pocket-knife.

He takes a few steps toward us, looking down as he cleans his nails with the knife.

A knife.

Several people gasp, and my mom blows a gasket.

"You son of a b–"

My heart lurches as Silas takes another threatening step toward my mom.

"Care to finish that sentence, Mrs. Rose?" He gives

her a feline smile as her face blanches. Her lips form a thin line, and she backs up a few steps. "I didn't think so. Now, go back to your fancy hotel and leave my employee the fuck alone."

His words shock me, not just because he threatened my mom with a *knife*–a fucking knife–but because he stood up for me.

No one, besides maybe Mindy, has ever stood up for me. My heart beats calm as my mom harrumphs and stalks off, casting a hateful glance in my direction before lifting her chin. I listen to the sound of her heels as she walks away, not daring to look at the guys.

I stare at the ground, my chest burning with emotion, and then I feel a warm hand on my shoulder.

"Hey," Damon says, his arched, scythe eyebrows furrowing slightly. "Let's go."

I look up at him, then at Silas and Jude. The crowd that had gathered thankfully disappeared with my mom. I guess they didn't want to get on Silas's bad side, either. I expect to see pity on their faces.

Pity... like on graduation night.

Instead, I just see fury. And a wrathful stillness that terrifies me. Especially radiating from Jude, who looks almost *too* serene for it to be real.

I look back up at Damon. His eyes are still narrowed in anger, but they're a bit softer now, and they twinkle slightly when I make eye contact.

"Why?" I ask as we slowly walk back to Savage Ink.

"We heard you crying earlier," Jude answers me, his

voice cool, smooth. I can feel him staring at my swollen face. When my eyes meet his, instead of the normal light brown color, they're glowing nearly fiery orange with rage.

sixteen

Jude

I'm still shaking as we step over the threshold into Savage. I mumble something about the restroom, and then I make my way to the back, closing the bathroom door behind me. Before I know what I'm doing, my fist is shattering the mirror, and my knuckles are bloodied. Panting, I wipe the sweat from my brow with my clean hand, and then I rinse my cut-up hand under the water, wincing as shards of glass scrape against my already tender flesh.

"Jude?"

Lennon's soft voice causes me to still. "I'll be right out."

I dry my hand off with a few paper towels, and then I reach up to the storage cabinet and pull out our neglected first aid kit. Ripping open a few band aid packages, I cover as much of the cuts as I can. Enough to disguise them until I can pull the black, latex gloves over them. Rinsing off the sink, I glance up at the broken mirror and shrug. I swing the door open, and Lennon's eyes immediately go to my hand.

"What happened?" She looks behind me. "Jesus Christ, Jude. Did you just–"

I push her against the wall, placing my bad hand next to her head. Her eyes widen as she takes in the blood seeping out of the too-small bandages.

"Just because we were nice to you back there doesn't mean we're friends."

The words feel less powerful today for some reason, but I appreciate the look of confusion on her face. *Good.* Wouldn't want her to get too comfortable.

"Jude, I–"

"You seem to have the same problem as your mother," I comment, smirking. A fresh batch of anger works its way through me at the mention of her mother, and I need to take it out on someone. "Mind your own fucking business and get back to work."

Her eyes penetrate mine with such intensity that I have to look away.

Fuck her.

Without another word, I leave her there.

I can feel Lennon's eyes burning through the back of my head for several minutes, and when I finally manage to look up again, she's unscrewing the broken mirror from the bathroom wall.

seventeen

Lennon

By the time the last customer leaves at around two in the morning, I'm nearly wringing my hands with anticipation and nervousness. I knew this was coming, and I've thought long and hard about it all evening. Seeing Jude–hell, seeing *Silas* threaten my mom like that–it undid something inside of me, and all I currently feel is remorse and guilt. They saved me back there, stood up for me, and protected me–and what had I done to them all those years ago? I'd lied. I'd accused them of something they never did, and it cost all of them so much.

Just as Silas begins to pack his things away, I walk up to his station.

"Wait." I try to get the words out before I chicken out. "Do me."

He raises his eyebrows, and Damon snorts from a few feet away.

"Well, princess, you're not really my type, but–"

I swallow the strange sting of rejection. Why should I care about that?

I roll my eyes and brush off his comment. "No, I mean... give me a tattoo."

Silas's blue eyes bore into mine, and my stomach clenches as his tongue swirls around the inside of his cheek.

"Are you going to pay me for this tattoo?" he asks, cocking his head and leaning back. "Or are you just demanding something from me?"

I narrow my eyes. "As payback," I explain, shuffling my feet. "Like what you did to Noah," I whisper.

His face falls, and the amusement dies as he frowns. "Noah is a rapist."

"And I am a bully," I say boldly. "I'd rather not wake up to you guys tying me up one night, so just get it over with now."

He considers it for a few seconds, and I look at Jude and Damon, who are both watching us raptly. I have no idea if that was their plan, or if I was even on their radar like that. My cheeks heat as I consider the fact that they really *don't* care. Maybe I'm putting my foot in my mouth yet again and being presumptuous.

"Okay, deal," Silas says slowly, his expression unmoving. He nudges his jaw to the chair, gesturing for me to sit. "Where?"

I don't move, instead swallowing nervously. "You choose."

My whole body is screaming that this is a bad idea.

He gives me a small smile, and I hear Damon and Jude continue to clean up their sections while pretending not to eavesdrop.

"Lie down," Silas commands, running a hand through his messy hair. He prepares his station, and as he lowers me down to a laying position, I close my eyes and clasp my hands together.

I don't want him to see me shaking.

Taking a few steadying breaths, I jump when the tattoo gun buzzes.

Silas chuckles. "Just warming her up," he says smoothly. His voice sends shivers down my spine, and I don't hate the feeling of the adrenaline coursing through me.

"Last chance, princess," he mumbles, and I snap my eyes open.

He's staring down at me, tattoo gun in his grasp, gloved hands gripping the stainless steel firmly. His lips are cracked from the long night, and his eyes are slightly rimmed with red. Still, he gives me a large smile, and I'm not sure if he's being nice or malicious.

"I'm not scared." I close my eyes again.

"You sure? I can see you shaking from here."

"Try this." Jude's voice is close, and when I open my eyes, he's holding a bottle of tequila. "And this." In his other hand is a soda can. "Two shots. Enough to relax you, but not enough to bleed all over Silas's station."

I squint and narrow my eyes. "Bleed all over?" My heart begins to race as I sit up and grab the two drinks, taking two large swigs and washing them both down with soda. I make a face and wipe my mouth with the back of my hand. Lying back down, I try not to gag.

"If you have too much alcohol in your system, it thins your blood," Silas explains. His voice is so low, it almost always sounds like a growl.

"Lovely," I whisper, squeezing my eyes shut, but I can already feel the alcohol doing its job. My body loosens, like coils softening, and I sort of feel like I'm floating. Jude was right–I'm not drunk. Just... at ease.

"Do you want me to tell you where–" Silas starts.

"Nope," I cut him off. "Just get it over with." My skin tingles, awareness spreading everywhere as I realize he must still be watching me. I peek between my lashes. He's frowning again, this time looking grumpy and perplexed at the same time. "Silas."

My voice wakes him from his stupor because he scowls down at me. "This might hurt," is all he says, and after I close my eyes fully, he unbuttons my shorts, exposing my purple underwear. Another shiver works down my spine at his touch. His gloved fingers snag my skin, but I can feel the warmth of his flesh through the material. I inhale deeply as he moves the fabric down my hips, and with each tug, something unexpected happens to my core–and the spot between my legs.

Well, princess, you're not really my type...

I ignore the way I'm disappointed that he said that. It

doesn't matter. I'm not interested, so why should I care if he isn't?

He rubs my hip bone for several seconds, the cold antibacterial wipe causing goosebumps to erupt everywhere. And then he blows cool air on that sensitive, wet part of me, and I nearly jump out of my seat.

"Whoa, there," he purrs, and I ignore it. *All of it.*

The way his voice is low and velvety, the smell of his skin and the rubber of the gloves, the way his fingers keep brushing that part of my lower abdomen–and the way that I can hear him breathing.

"Buckle up," he warns quietly, and I hiss as the needle hits my skin.

"Ow," I whine, and Damon and Jude chuckle in the background. "Oh, you're one to talk, Jude," I mutter, and I hear Damon cover his laugh with a cough. "Let's see all of your tattoos," I add, feeling very high and mighty.

"Oh, I have tattoos, Lennon," he utters, his voice sounding sensuous. "If you're lucky, maybe I'll let you see them up close."

I squeeze my legs together, and somehow, I'm imagining his... thing. He has tattoos down... there? What are they? Why there? What do they look like?

Silas is gentle enough as he works. The burning sensation of the needle gives way to a tickling one, and I grind my jaw to keep from making any noises. Several minutes pass, and I see him pick up a few different colors. Each time he starts again, each time he inks me after taking a small break, my whole body shivers ever so slightly. It feels like my skin is on fire in the best way possible. I squirm in my chair, trying to get rid of the tension building up. I want to scream, and it's starting to feel really good.

"Nearly done," Silas tells me, and in some sick, twisted way, I am disappointed with that fact. "You did well," he adds lightly, and I hear him turn the gun off. I open my eyes, squinting at the brightness of the light above us.

"It looks so much more painful in the movies," I comment, my hands shaking with adrenaline. I feel like I could run a thousand miles. "That was... incredible."

I can't stop smiling as Silas dabs my sore hip bone a few times. I see him wipe it down once more, and then he picks up some antibiotic ointment. I try not to moan as his fingers lightly dab the sore area. *Why am I having this reaction?* It's almost like I'm... turned on. He opens a bandage and places it over the ink. I assume he chose a horrendous font, and I have zero desire to actually see it, so I let him cover it up without looking.

"Keep this on for twelve hours," he says as he moves my chair to a seated position. "After twelve hours, wash with antibacterial soap three times a day, and follow up with fragrance-free lotion." He furrows his brows. "And do not pick at it when it scabs over."

I nod, trying to remember the same instructions *I've* been telling clients with this unexpected rush of excitement flowing through me. "Okay, sure." I look down at the bandage. "Is it... horrible?"

He snaps his gloves off and discards them, crossing his arms. I ignore the way it pushes his muscles up and out, or the way his ink looks against his black t-shirt, contrasting with his golden skin.

"It's exactly what I would've chosen for you."

I digest his words for a few seconds, and his eyes don't leave mine. "Oh... so, that bad, huh?"

He smirks. "Just be patient and don't peek until tomorrow."

I nod and stand, suddenly feeling slightly woozy. Silas reaches a hand out and helps me balance myself.

"The adrenaline will trick you," he murmurs, low enough for only me to hear. "It'll make you want to run and scream and fuck, all at the same time."

Lord, the way he says *fuck–*

"Emphasis on the fucking," he adds, and I swallow as my heart thumps against my ribs. My breath catches, and my lips part slightly as he leans in. "That's why you can barely stand."

I take a step away and nod once, completely thrown off by his closeness, delicately pulling my shorts back up and buttoning them. "It's a good thing I'm not your type, then."

He gives me a look of confusion, but then realization hits, and I can see him about to explain himself. So, I speak before he can.

"I should go." I turn on my heel too quickly, stumbling a step, then walk toward the desk with determination to get out of here.

My hip aches now, and seemingly out of nowhere, I

feel really stupid for going through with this. I grab my purse and head to the door. *What was I thinking?* I just let Silas Huxley tattoo me. It probably says *whore* instead of *bully*, or something far worse. My throat seems to be closing with my nerves, so I wave goodbye without another word before pushing the door open.

Gulping the refreshing summer night air, I turn right and push the door to my stairs open.

Stupid.

Maybe my mom was right. What the hell am I doing working at a place like this? I'm getting swept up into God knows what, with guys who confuse the hell out of me. I mean, take Jude for example–stoic, quiet, cruel–yet he punched a mirror for me. *Because* of me. He didn't admit it, but he went right to the bathroom after the confrontation with my mother. He was angry–*for me.* They act like they hate me, but... after today, I'm not so sure. If they wanted me gone so badly, they would've let me go to the Four Seasons with my mom. Instead, they stood up for me.

Like friends.

I shake my head as I let myself into my apartment. Changing quickly, I don't dare peek at the bandage, instead throwing on a camisole and loose sleep shorts. I brush my teeth, wash my face, and crawl into bed. Just as I pull the covers over myself, there's a knock at my front door.

A cold sweat breaks out along my skin. Who the hell is knocking on my door at three-thirty in the morning? I stand up and slowly walk to the door. God, I wish I were rich enough for one of those video doorbells. Maybe I will buy myself one if I end up staying here. My heart races inside of my chest, and I sneak a quick peek out of the peephole.

"Silas?" I ask, swinging the door open. "What are you–"

He rushes in, pressing me against the wall behind me. I gasp, but my body explodes with heat as he pins my hands at my sides. *Jesus Christ–*

"For the record," he says roughly, the scent of beer on his breath. "I never said you weren't my type, Lennon Rose." My name sounds harsh coming from his lips, but in an oddly familiar way. Like that's the only way he knows how to say my name.

After hating me for fourteen years.

My breathing turns ragged as he presses himself against me–*all* of himself. Which includes something large and hard against my stomach.

"What I meant was, you're not really my type, but explain to me why I haven't stopped thinking about you since you arrived back in Greythorn?" My heart is pounding, and my blood rushes in my eardrums at his admission. "And if the women I have dated are any indication, perhaps I *shouldn't* have a type." He leans down, his blue eyes twinkling. I inhale sharply when he presses himself against me again. "I'm not thinking about them, though, Lennon. I'm thinking about the leggy blonde who just moved in upstairs," he breaths, almost angrily. "The one I'm supposed to hate."

I shake my head. "Silas, I'm–"

He takes a step back, and the cool air where his body once was is startling. I almost reach out for him, but then I think better of it.

"Goodnight, Lennon." He turns and walks back out through the open door.

eighteen

Lennon

I wake up late the next morning, my brain foggy and my mouth dry. I slowly crawl out of bed, stumbling and nearly falling over before reaching for my dresser to steady myself. The motion makes me wince, and my fingers graze the bandage on my hip bone just as the events of last night flood my mind. First, the tattoo, and then Silas showing up here and admitting he can't stop thinking about me...

The thoughts cause me to shake my head as I make my way to the bathroom. I grimace as I see my reflection–wild hair, smudged mascara, and as I lift my shirt and lower my shorts, a bandage covering my right hip area. I sigh and splash some water on my face. *Why did I get a tattoo? Who am I?* I dry my face off and brush my teeth, delaying the inevitable. The clock on my phone says it's just past eleven, so technically, it hasn't been a full twelve hours, but the morbid curiosity is almost too much to bear. Once I rinse my mouth out, I reach down and slowly peel the bandage off, holding my breath.

Whore, bully, bitch...

Those are the words I expect to see. It takes me a second to realize what I'm seeing, and at first, I think he must've made a mistake. But then realization hits, and I gasp.

The Savage Ink logo, with the words wrapped around a heart, and a knife about to plunge into the heart.

He fucking *branded* me.

With shaking hands, I twist around and grab my phone and keys. I don't care that I'm in pajama shorts and a very thin camisole. I don't bother smoothing my hair or putting on shoes. Instead, I throw my door open and stomp downstairs, turning left when I get outside. Cupping my face against the window of Savage Ink, I see that it's closed, and no one is inside as I should have expected.

There are a couple of IPA bottles on the coffee table, though, which tells me Silas *had* been drinking last night. I let out an exasperated groan, turning around quickly and nearly falling backwards as I bump into–

"You," I seethe, looking up at Silas.

He seems surprised to see me, and before he can respond, his eyes narrow as they rove over my chest, and eventually, my exposed lower stomach. It's obvious the bandage is off now.

"It hasn't been twelve hours," he remarks, his voice frustrated and rough.

"Why?" I let out a spiteful laugh and lower my shorts a bit. "I'm not a cow," I hiss. "You can't just brand me like swine." Silas takes a step back and observes me, a cocky smirk on his lips. My chest rises and falls as I take in his aviator sunglasses, denim shirt, and ripped black jeans. I pull my shorts up more and wrap my arms around myself. "It doesn't make sense. You all hate me–"

"If you really think we ever hated you, you weren't paying attention." I let out an annoyed huff, but before I can respond, he chuckles as he walks over and opens the door to Savage Ink. "Actually, I'm pretty sure Jude hated you there for a while."

I follow him inside and he turns to face me after the door closes. "Is this all a joke to you?" I ask, shoving against his firm chest. "Hire me, humiliate me, and then fucking *mark* me like that–"

"You're so quick to point fingers, Lennon." I go to respond, but he places a hand on my mouth. All I can taste is salt, and his callouses from the tattoo gun are rough on my morning-chapped lips. "Think back to that night," he says gently. I make a sound against his hand, but he holds it against me firmer, backing me up against the glass door. "You know which night I'm talking about. We were trying to help you. We were always trying to help you. But like a shelter dog, you just wanted to bite us." He removes his hand and then his sunglasses, pocketing them before pulling his lower lip into his mouth. His eyebrows furrow slightly as he cocks his head.

"Maybe I did want a little bit of revenge with the tattoo." He smirks, glancing down at the sliver of exposed skin again. "I don't know why I did it. I guess I just wanted you to think of us whenever you see it. Think of *me*."

I open and close my mouth, but he's rendered me speechless.

"The tattoo," he interrupts, brushing the back of his hand against my jawline, "is a reminder for you. Not for us. For you." His gaze glides down to my feet, then back up, and he touches my fresh ink again, making my nipples peak beneath my shirt. "That maybe all along, we were the good guys. That maybe you fit in here–at Savage. With us." I open my mouth to moan, but he places his hand gently on my lips again. "Don't make the sound I think you were just about to make," he says gruffly. "It'd be an invitation to keep touching you, and I have a lot of things to do today."

My body sparks with fire, and when he drops his hand, I take a step back.

"Well, I guess, thank you for not tattooing 'whore' on my cheek," I joke, trying to dispel the uneasiness coursing through me with his kind words.

He smiles, and his dark, contemplative gaze teases me. "I won't go easy on you next time."

I bite the inside of my cheek as I look down. "Next time?"

He smirks. "There's always a next time when it comes to getting a tattoo."

I tamp my smile down. "Okay, well, see you tonight."

"We're closed tonight."

I rear my head back. "Closed? I didn't realize the shop was closed on Sundays."

He rubs his mouth. "We're having a party later. You should come."

I narrow my eyes, scanning his face for any insincerity. A small part of me thinks this whole thing–him being nice–is a prank.

"A party? Where?" I uncross my arms, and Silas's eyes take that as an invitation to glance over my chest once again.

His tongue rolls around the inside of his cheek as he tilts his head. "My house."

I stand a bit straighter. "The house you grew up in?"

He smirks. "I never did get to show you the chapel in high school."

An eerie chill works down my spine at his words. "Yeah, well, we weren't exactly friends in high school," I retort.

He nods and looks down, a smile tugging at his lips. Is he...*flirting*?

"You made damn well sure we weren't, Lennon Rose." As he looks up, his light blue eyes bore into mine. He reaches into his pocket and hands me a wad of cash. "I forgot to pay you last night. We should probably set up a direct deposit for you. I fucking hate handling cash."

And then he walks away, and I look down at the money.

"Silas, this is five hundred dollars," I say, my tone higher in pitch than I intended. I tally up the money he's already given me. "You're overpaying me."

He doesn't say anything as he begins to clean up the beer bottles and mess from last night. I look down at the money and take three hundred out, placing it on the table.

"I wouldn't do that," he warns from right behind me, making me jump. "Take the damn money, Lennon."

I shake my head. "No. It's too much–"

"I'm trying to give you a way out of that apartment." His voice is hoarse. "I know you want to break ties with your mom. Let us help you."

First the garbage can, then the graduation party...

We were trying to help you.

We were always trying to help you.

But like a shelter dog, you just wanted to bite us.

I take the money and nod once. It's not enough. I'm not sure I'll ever feel like it's enough to repay them. But if helping me makes them feel good...

We saw you.

We see you.

"Thank you," I say clearly.

He turns and walks away. "See you tonight."

nineteen

Lennon

On a whim, I text Lola to see if she wants to come to the party, and to my surprise, she was already planning on going. She agrees to pick me up at nine, and I try not to roll my eyes at the lateness of it all. Wright and I were usually in bed by nine, so staying up late like this is a whole new world for me.

I change into a new outfit of faux leather leggings, black stilettos, and an oversized band tee that I've had forever. I treated myself to a few new things today from one of the local boutiques, and it feels nice to dress up a bit. I curl my hair in loose waves and add some smokey eyeshadow to my lids, and then a minute before nine, Lola texts me that she's parked out front. Grabbing my purse, I do a onceover in the mirror, taking a deep breath. Butterflies flit through my stomach, making me feel anxious about tonight. I shake the feelings away as I lock up and head down to Lola's car.

"Well," I say, chuckling as I open the passenger door, "I did *not* expect you to drive a Tesla."

She laughs, and I look over at her. Black boots, baggy, ripped jeans, and a cropped flannel shirt. Her long black hair is pulled back into a low bun, and she's the only person I know who can pull off black lipstick.

"Yeah, it was my husband's Christmas present." She nods to the back. "Don't be too impressed. I'm still a mom, and the backseat is full of old cheerios and cheese."

I smile as I buckle up and we drive away. "Thanks for picking me up."

"Sure. I'm not far. We live in the condos just outside of town," she explains. "We make do here, but the plan is to move to Boston soon and open a bakery in the Brighton area. I'd love to live in the city, and to possibly afford something bigger for my daughter."

"How old is she?"

Lola smiles. "Three. She's adorable but also a bit of a nightmare right now, so I'm glad to be getting out of the house." She turns to face me. "How has it been at Savage?"

I shrug. "Good. It's been nice to get out and have some stability." I don't mention the bathroom or bubblegum cleanings as I have a feeling Lola would *not* approve. "How long have you and your husband been married?"

She snorts with a grin. "Fifteen years." I raise my

eyebrows, trying to determine her age. "Yeah, we were young and stupid. And we were *really* stupid until a few years ago, when we both got sober. No drugs or alcohol for nearly five years. And then we popped out a kid, and he became a firefighter..." She trails off, her grin widening. "I love my life, man. I worked hard for it. I'm glad we waited to have kids until we got our shit together. I'm proud of how we parent her."

I smile. "I'm proud of you and your husband," I say honestly. "A lot of parents have kids without realizing they need to be present for them."

Lola glances over at me, but I look down and swallow. She must know not to pry, because she changes the subject.

"Are the guys treating you nicely?"

Again, I don't go into detail as I answer. "Yeah. They're moody, but overall, they're nice."

If you don't count how they dragged me into a dark alley and proceeded to tattoo Noah Adelmann's forehead... or how they branded me.

"They're good guys. They're the reason Sam and I got clean." I open my mouth to ask how, but we stop at a light and she turns to face me fully. "So, Lennon Rose. What *really* brings you back to Greythorn?"

I pick at a loose thread on the hem of my shirt as I contemplate how to explain the last ten years of my life, how to sum it up in the next few minutes. But does the beginning even matter? College, various retail jobs, getting engaged to Wright, moving into his penthouse, becoming a stay-at-home girlfriend... none of that mattered, because it didn't really feel like me anymore. Sure, it was my life, but I'd grown a lot these last two weeks. I've discovered what I like and don't like, and how I *don't* want my life to be. I didn't realize until just now that I have my mom's same Diane von Furstenberg wrap dress in a different pattern, hanging in the closet at Wright's house.

If I stayed in that situation, I would've turned into my mom.

"My fiancé cheated on me with his assistant, so I left. Came back home to Greythorn, and now I'm staying above Savage Ink."

I don't bring up that my mom owns it–the whole building, actually. It's embarrassing to admit the amount of wealth I grew up with. Luckily, Lola doesn't ask about that.

"Damn. How long were you guys together?"

I swallow. "Ten years."

She whistles. "Fuck. What a prick." Turning to look at me, she smiles. "You seem okay, though, right?"

I smile. "Yeah. He was bad in bed."

We both laugh as she turns down one of the residential streets, and I immediately recognize the stately house before us. Silas Huxley's house was notorious growing up, and a small part of me is eager to see what all the fuss is about. I'd heard rumors of a prison cell in one of the closets, a basement chapel, and that his parents made everyone who entered the house take communion. He was never allowed to attend birthday parties, and we certainly never came here growing up, either.

The house is made of dark wood, and the curved driveway is empty. There are no lights on, and a shiver works down my spine as Lola parks in front of the large door with iron fixtures. It looks more like a church than a house, and I climb out as Lola swears under her breath.

"I swear to God, this place is haunted as fuck."

I don't say anything as we walk up to the door, and she pushes it open. "What happened to his parents?" I ask, looking around.

"They got wrapped up in some freaky cult, completely lost it, and went totally mad. They're locked up somewhere, and Silas inherited the house because they're unfit to even make the mortgage payments." She cocks her head and narrows her eyes at me. "Between you and me, there's a lot of other shit that happened, but I won't get into it now."

My blood cools as we make our way through the dark house. "Doesn't seem like anyone is here."

She chuckles. "They're down in the chapel, most likely."

I stop walking, ignoring the walls of crosses and black furniture. "So it's true? There *is* a chapel in the basement?"

She smirks. "Hell yeah. Come on, let's go."

She leads me to the kitchen, and from there, opens a door I wouldn't have even known existed. Voices float up to us, and I follow her down a narrow, curved stairway, gawking as we enter a small, cavernous... *chapel.* Wood-paneled walls, a few rows of pews, and a legitimate altar at the front of the room. My eyes snap to the people seated in the pews drinking beer–a few guys and girls I don't know, along with Silas, Damon, and Jude, who are all watching me as I walk farther into the dimly-lit basement.

My skin tingles as I wave and smile. "Hi," I say shyly.

"I'm fucking starving," Lola whines, setting her purse down. "Can I grab something to eat?"

Silas waves her off and smiles as she goes, and I look between the three of them. Jude is the first to speak.

"We didn't think you'd show."

I stand up taller. "I expected a crowded party," I huff, shrugging. "I thought perhaps I could disappear into anonymity if it sucked." A few people laugh, and Damon chokes on his beer. "This is like a high school sleepover," I tease with a smirk.

"The real party hasn't started," Silas explains, leaning back against a pew. "You tell me if it feels like a sleepover once it starts."

I nod, shifting my weight from one hip to the other. "Where's the beer?" I ask, and before anyone can answer, Damon hops up.

"Come on. I'll grab a beer for everyone," he says, looking at Silas and Jude.

I walk up the stairs ahead of him, very aware of the fact that his face is at ass-level. I almost say something about it, but he walks past me to the fridge when we get to the kitchen. Lola is hovering over the island, inhaling what looks like a burrito.

"Sure thing, Lo. Help yourself." He places a hand on her back as he passes her. His tone is teasing, but it's full of warmth.

"I can't wait for the day you have a toddler, Brooks. You just wait. You eat, sleep, shit, and fuck whenever and wherever you get an opportunity, okay?"

He laughs, and I smile. Grabbing four beers in one hand, he closes the fridge and turns to me, handing me one of them and gesturing to the bottle opener laying on the island.

I take all four beers and open them, and when I look up, he's watching me with a darkened expression.

"What?" I ask, acutely aware of the fact that Lola must've gone downstairs because she's no longer in the kitchen.

His eyes unabashedly rove down my body and back up, and he gives me an appreciative smile.

"Nothing, princess. You just look really fucking hot tonight." My stomach bottoms out at his words, and I can't help but admire the way he looks, too. Black trousers, a green and blue flannel shirt, and his dark brown eyes and dark lashes contrast against the bright kitchen light. He lowers his head a bit as he takes three of the beers from me, and his fingers brush mine briefly as I hand them back. "I'm still getting used to the idea of being attracted to Lennon Rose."

"Thanks, I think," I joke, taking a sip of beer and avoiding eye contact.

"Why do you do that?" Damon asks, his voice softer.

I snap my eyes to his. "Do what?"

"You have these walls erected around yourself, and any time anyone says or does something nice, you respond with humor or anger."

My cheeks flush because I know he's right. "I don't know, honestly. I guess I'm still trying to come to terms with the fact that you guys don't hate me. The kindness throws me off."

"Kindness?" he asks, trailing a finger down my bare arm. "You think we're being kind?"

I shrug, ignoring the way my skin pebbles at his touch. "I don't know–"

"Would someone *nice* say that they want to fuck you, Lennon?"

I keep my breathing even as heat flares through me. "What makes you think you even have the chance to fuck me?" I ask, taking a swig of my beer to calm my nerves and leaning against the counter.

He smiles and takes a step closer. "Trust me, Lennon..." He trails off, lifting my chin with his free hand. His eyes, they're so dark, they're nearly black. I could stare into them for hours, days even. His wild, dark hair is swept up into an artful mess atop his head, and he smells like cherries. "If I wanted you, I could have you."

"Is that a threat?" As the words leave my mouth, in the tone that they do, I realize I'm flirting.

My eyes stay locked on his, trying to seem completely unfazed by the lust rushing through me.

"I'd sit you up on this counter and fuck you so hard that you'd forget what day it is," he says, his voice low and rough. "I wouldn't be gentle. Do you still think I'm being *kind*?"

Just as I open my mouth, Lola comes back into the kitchen. "Do you guys have any more of that guacamole?" she asks, setting down a glass of water.

Damon shakes his head and takes a step away from me, flicking his tongue between two fingers and winking before turning to Lola.

I'm not repulsed in the slightest, instead I try not to notice how long his tongue is...

"There was a whole bowl in there. Look in the back."

She grunts and ruffles through the fridge, so comfortable here–in this house, and with them. So they can't be complete asses.

"You guys all live here?" I ask. I'd never thought of their living situation. I guess I always assumed they still had apartments in Boston.

"Temporarily," Damon muses, turning and walking back toward the door to the basement. He looks at me over his shoulder. "Let's go."

twenty

Silas

Lennon and Damon walk down the stairs just as I'm setting up my station. Smirking, I lay Fran down on a pew so that she's on her stomach, and Lennon's eyes widen when she realizes that Fran is topless.

I look down at Fran and clean her back off–first with a wet wipe, and then an antibacterial wipe. I see Jude hovering over Ben, his tattoo gun already in his hand. A couple of Ben's friends are smoking a joint, and Fran's partner, Avery, is near her feet, rubbing them. When I glance back up at Lennon, she's still standing by the stairs. Her eyes meet mine, and I smile.

"Still look like a sleepover to you?"

She shakes her head, and her hand brushes her hip bone. "I'm not sure yet."

Jude snorts. "Take a seat. I'll give you a go with the gun if you want."

Lennon stills. "The–the gun?"

Ben looks at Lennon with a hungry expression, his eyes traveling down her mile long legs, and something hot and possessive works through me.

"Don't even think about it," I growl, and he turns to face me. "You fucking touch her, and you're a dead man."

Lennon frowns as she sits near me, and I begin on Fran's back. As I go through the movements, I explain to Lennon about how we have these parties sometimes, where our friends willingly act as the canvases for the things we want to create. Sometimes the mundaneness of owning a tattoo shop really takes the creative edge off of everything, and we use these nights to fill our artistic wells again. She just watches us as we work, and soon, Damon takes his place behind Avery and begins to ink the back of her hand.

The night wears on, and after a couple more beers on Lennon's part, she kicks her shoes off and begins to talk with Lola and one of Ben's friends. I keep my eye on them, nearly messing up Fran's back in the process. Damon and Jude must feel the same way I do, because Jude excuses himself and says something to Lennon, whispering in her ear before heading upstairs.

I try not to smile as she follows him.

I don't think any of us will be able to keep our hands off her tonight.

Not with the way those pants sculpt her ass, the leather clinging to her long, toned legs.

Or the way her pink lips seem to call to us like a mythological siren.

I don't know what changed recently, but I do know that all of us can feel the frenetic and erratic energy whenever she's in the room.

And I don't think any of us would ever be willing to ignore it for the sake of the others.

twenty-one

Lennon

It's sheer curiosity that has me following Jude up the stairs. He hadn't said anything particularly captivating. There wasn't some magical sentence that lured me. He'd only commented that Ben and his friends couldn't stop staring at me. But it was the *way* he said it. The way anger tinged his words, and laced around his tongue as he gritted them out, that made me pause for a minute before heading upstairs to see if he was okay. And now I'm stalking through the creepy Huxley house alone, looking for the most unhinged of the three of them in an unfamiliar, dark place.

The get-together is interesting–small, intimate, and casual. All three guys are inking their friends with things that don't align with their normal styles, and I have to wonder if this is the only time they get to act like true artists. All three of them are freehanding the ink, meaning they aren't using any stencils or mockups, so their art is messier than normal.

I personally think it's beautiful, because it shows their true talent. It's as if they are sketching on a piece of paper. And the things they're sketching? *Gorgeous.* Colorful, abstract, sweeping art. Stuff you'd see in a modern art museum. And nothing was discussed beforehand. It's just art on skin, and these people are letting the guys do it to them, because they trust them.

I walk up the grand staircase made entirely of black marble, and goosebumps erupt along my skin when I think of growing up in a place like this. There are no signs of life anywhere, and this is no place for growing boys. It's like Silas and his brother grew up living in purgatory, unable to get any warmth from their home or their parents.

Perhaps Silas and I have more in common than I thought.

I walk down the long hallway, passing a room that must be Damon's, because it smells like ripe cherries. He has navy sheets on his king-sized bed, dark wood furniture, and a fur rug on the floor. It's messy and dark–exactly the kind of room I would've pictured for him. Making my way down the hallway, I pass a bathroom, and office, and then I stop in front of what must be the master bedroom.

I push the door open and realize this is Silas's room. A black, ornate, wooden bed with neutral bedding sits in the center, surrounded by Victorian furniture with a steampunk twist, and a black and white rug on the floor. I wander over to the sprawling desk next to the balcony door, and I nearly gasp. Notebook after notebook of drawings, charcoal and pencil, of anything and everything. Flowers, faces, houses, maps, and then other, more abstract things that cause my hand to rub my throat as I swallow thickly. He's good. *Really* good. It's no wonder he's one of the most sought-after tattoo artists in the country. I turn to walk out of the room before anyone catches me snooping, and I head to the other side of the house with more bedrooms.

The first two are very clearly guest bedrooms, and then there's a library, a bathroom, and an entertainment room with a massive TV. I make it to the other side of the hallway, and there's one door left, sitting ajar.

I push it open, stunned when I see what can only be Jude's room. Tidy, white, minimalist. It's perfect, with a white, pristine bed, a red chair sitting at just the perfect angle in front of the window, a large, polished iMac computer in one corner, and a mid-century lamp that casts an eerie, orange glow throughout the room. This is a psychopath's room, for someone with too much time on their hands–someone who stays up late rearranging furniture and decluttering. It's *too* clean. I instantly feel myself breaking out in a cold sweat as I take a step back, but then I hear a small noise coming from the ensuite bathroom.

I ball my fists as I walk silently over the white shag rug toward the bathroom. Putting my ear against the closed door, I hear heavy breathing, and my heart slams against my chest.

I turn the handle slowly. As I push the door open a crack, I peek through the sliver and see Jude's back to me. He's panting, his muscled arms strained as one of them works something in front of him, and it only takes me a second to realize what he's doing. I gasp, and the noise causes him to turn around, which then causes me to push the door open farther, exposing him and–

Holy fuck.

I can't look away as he strokes his shaft, slower now that he has an audience. I can't look away, because even though he has zero ink on his body, his cock is covered in tats. And there are several piercings along the top in a row, neatly spaced out. *Seven.* There are seven. Like a ladder.

"Hello, Lennon," he says roughly, not even stopping.

"I–I'm–" I stutter, taking a step back.

"Where are you going?" he asks, gesturing for me to come closer. He tilts his head back, eyes looking up at the ceiling, bottom lip between his teeth as he pumps faster. Lowering his gaze back to me, he gives me a lecherous grin. "I was thinking about you, anyway."

I inhale sharply as he walks over to where I'm standing. I can smell the sweat on him, and the sound of him jerking himself, of the wetness along his thick, long shaft...

My clit throbs as he breathes heavily, inches from me. As I watch him, I can feel my face burning as my chest rises and falls rapidly. I should walk away. But his breathing is uneven, and then he lets out a low groan—a sound that travels from my ears straight to my core, making my clit pulse. I clamp my legs together and take a small step back.

My eyes travel down to his hips as they move into his hand now. He's properly *fucking* his own hand, and the motion of his hips is smooth, practiced. I close my eyes as I imagine what it would feel like for him to be moving that way on top of me. How he might hover over me and move his hips just so, just to achieve the right angle...

How he might tease me, thrusting into me and then pulling all the way out, his cocky smirk inches from my face as he watches me come undone.

I snap my eyes open when he moans again, my mouth parting as his hand flies up and down urgently. Everything inside of me is thrumming with unmet pleasure, and I realize I never did anything like this with Wright. It was always missionary, lights dimmed, jackhammer style. We never fooled around like this, even when I asked him to. Even when I *begged* him. I pull my lower lip between my teeth as I watch Jude fuck his own hand, watch as the head of his cock pumps between his clenched fingers, the tip dripping with precum.

"Fuck," he groans, his voice gravelly. "Watch me come, Lennon."

I look down as his shaft stiffens and hardens, watching with a pulsing cunt as he tips his head back and stops moving his hand altogether, letting his bouncing, throbbing cock come all over the floor and his hand.

His body jerks and shudders as some of it spurts onto my leggings.

"Fuck," he repeats, falling back against the counter.

I. Can't. Breathe.

"I'm sorry, I should go," I blurt out quickly, turning around. I'm a couple of feet away when I realize I don't want to leave.

That was the hottest thing I'd seen in a long time.

"Stop apologizing and look at me," he commands, and I twist around just as he zips himself up and walks over to me. Lifting the hand that he used to jack himself off, he reaches up and drags his thumb across my lower lip, smirking as I stiffen. The salty taste of him makes me squirm, and Jude just grins as he moves his thumb inside of my mouth. I close my lips around his skin and suck, and his hooded eyes nearly roll into the back of his head. I stifle a moan as his thumb works my tongue, and I swirl it around a bit, imagining it's another appendage. As quickly as he inserted it, he removes it, and I'm left wanting more.

I open my mouth to yell at him–for doing it or for stopping, I'm not sure–when he brushes past me. He leaves me alone in the bathroom, shaking, *wanting,* and nearly ready to explode.

twenty-two

Damon

Around midnight, Lola and Lennon leave our house, and Silas hasn't stopped glaring at Jude. Once Ben, Fran, and the gang leave, fresh ink all bandaged up, I slam the door shut and turn to Silas.

"What the fuck is wrong, dude?"

Silas' nostrils flare slightly as he sighs. "Ask him. He went upstairs with Lennon earlier, and she was all out of sorts afterwards."

I cross my arms and cock my head as my eyes land on Jude's smug face. "We're supposed to be fucking *with* her. Not fucking her."

I feel like a hypocrite saying that.

Jude gives me a small smile and rolls his tongue around inside his cheeks. Truth be told, the guy is terrifying sometimes. He's so calm, so collected.

Nothing ruffles his feathers. I've only ever seen him angry a handful of times. But he's fucked up in the mind. Something's not right up there. I love him to death, and he's like a brother to me, but I would not want to get on his bad side. He's capable of some Hannibal Lector shit.

"Who said I *didn't* fuck with her?"

"What did you do?" Silas asks.

I turn back to Silas. "Why do you care?"

He grimaces. "I don't care."

"Bullshit," Jude interjects, grinning. "I saw the way you watched her tonight. Just admit it."

Silas frowns and runs a hand through his hair. "She made my life hell. I can't just forget that."

"Can't you?" I add, playing devil's advocate. "She's obviously not the same person that she was. And for some fucking reason, unbeknownst to me, she seems to fit into our trio perfectly." Silas opens his mouth with a retort, but I shake my head. "You know it's true. Somewhere along the way, we stopped trying to get revenge. Inking her last night, inviting her tonight—standing up to her mom," I point out, glaring at Silas. "Can we all agree to call a truce? We're all ten years older."

Jude laughs, and I scowl at him. "Man, just tell us you want to fuck her."

"Do *you* both want to fuck her? Is that why you're acting psychotic?" Silas accuses, pointing a finger at Jude. "Admit it."

Jude chuckles darkly, crossing his arms as he looks down. "Look at the pot calling the kettle black."

I shake my head. "I don't know why we're arguing. She's definitely fuckable. We can all agree on that."

"I'm done with this conversation," Silas growls, turning around and heading to the back of the house.

Jude watches me with a curious expression, and I lean against the wall next to the door. "You going to tell me what you did to her?" I ask, narrowing my eyes.

Jude smiles innocently. "She walked in on me using the restroom. Nothing scandalous." He turns and walks away, and somehow, I know he's not telling me the whole truth.

twenty-three

Lennon

I wake up half past six the next morning after tossing and turning for hours. I don't really know what to think of what happened last night—of the guys, the party, and especially Jude. Just weeks ago, I would've found what he did insulting. But I'm not the same person now. I don't know Jude very well, and I don't think many people see all sides of him, but last night felt illicit in the best way possible. The way his corded arms looked as he gripped his shaft, the intrigue of his piercings... it was all new to me, but I wanted to know more.

I make myself a cup of coffee and open my computer. The first thing I do is count the cash I've accumulated since working at Savage Ink, adding it all up to estimate a monthly salary. Then, I begin to build a reasonable budget and savings plan. All of my subscriptions, insurance, and payments came out of my joint account with Wright, so I log in and remove his access to it, even though there's less than $100 left. I make a mental note to stop by the bank later to deposit my cash.

Last, I begin to search for apartments in Greythorn and the surrounding areas. My first priority is getting out of this place and into my own rental. I remember Lola mentioning last night that they lived in some condo complex in Greythorn, so I send her a text asking her to let me know if she sees anything open in the near future. I scan the other listings, but most of them are rooms in giant mansions. Sighing, I shut my computer and stand to get ready for the day. I clean my tattoo and shower, and by the time I'm done, it's nearly nine in the morning. I throw on a pair of shorts, a cropped tank, and sneakers, then head outside.

The morning is hot as I make my way to Romancing the Bean. It was my favorite place to go as a teenager—a cute café with delicious pastries and coffee. I order a chocolate croissant and a coffee, then head into the central park to eat and people watch, choosing a bench that faces the trees. I stuff my face with the warm croissant, and then I smile when I think of last night, catching myself before I look like a fool.

Ten years ago, I never could've imagined enjoying my time with Silas Huxley, Damon Brooks, and Jude Vanderbilt. Especially not after *that* night. I always wanted to reach out, wanted to ask if they were okay after I went home. But I never worked up the courage to do so. I just assumed I'd never see them again, but here we all were, back in Greythorn and working together.

I walk home slowly, finishing my coffee and basking in the warm sunshine. It's humid, and I'm already sweating profusely, but I can't help but love summertime. New England can be so dreary in the winter, so I really try to savor the sun whenever it comes out in the summer months. I feel a small smile starting to stretch my lips, when someone shouts my name from across the street.

I hardly recognize him at first, and it takes him crossing the street and jogging up to me for me to realize it's the man from the bar on Friday. In the daylight, he seems younger somehow, with black and silver-tinged hair, tan skin, and green eyes. He must be at least fifty, and as he gets closer, I see that his forehead is uneven and scarred. I didn't notice that in the dimness of the bar. His eyes twinkle as he takes me in, and I cock my head and keep my smile in place as he saunters up to me.

"Lennon," he muses, grinning as he continues to check me out. "The mystery girl from the bar."

Listen, Lennon. You need to be careful. Those guys are unhinged.

A sudden wave of protectiveness washes over me, and I take a step back. "Yep, it's me," I say, trying to keep my face neutral.

"Still working for those psychos at Savage Ink?" he asks.

I look up at him, shielding my face from the sun. "Yup."

He takes a step forward, and I'm instantly uncomfortable. Outwardly, he seems very nice—warm voice, soft eyes... but *something* about him gives me the creeps.

"Come work for me instead," he offers, holding out a business card. "I can pay you double what those scumbags are paying you."

I open and close my mouth, unsure of how to process what he's offering me. I take the card from him and look down at it, but it's only a name and a number.

Liam James.

I hand the card back. "I like working at Savage Ink. Thank you for the offer, though."

His eyes flash with something that makes me stumble back a step. My instincts aren't wrong, then.

"You're making a mistake. Take it from me, I've known Silas Huxley his whole life. He got mixed up with bad people from a young age, and so did his brother. I'm trying to help you before you make the same mistake."

A few people stare at us as they walk by, and I narrow my eyes at Liam. "*How* do you know Silas?"

He stands up a bit straighter. "I was good friends with his parents."

I think of Lola's words from last night. *They got wrapped up in some freaky cult, completely lost it, and went totally mad.*

I study the way his shirt is too neat, too tidy, and the way he continues to encroach on my space.

"I'm sorry. I should get back." I'm suddenly aware that he might see where I live if I walk home now. I'm only a block away. *Please, let someone be at Savage Ink...* "Nice to meet you, Liam." *Not.*

He doesn't say anything as I walk back toward Savage Ink, my hands shaking slightly from the encounter. *What the hell is his deal, and why does he hate Silas and the guys so much?*

I don't look behind me as I walk up to Savage Ink, and the door is propped open. I breathe a sigh of relief and walk inside.

"Hi," I say breathlessly, looking around. But there's no one here. "Hello?"

Goosebumps cover my skin when I see Liam walk by slowly. His eyes meet mine for a second as he, too, realizes that I'm alone in here. I give him a quick smile to appease him, and he just stops and watches me as I pretend to sort the business cards.

"What the fuck is Liam James doing here?" Damon asks from behind me, making me jump two feet in the air.

"Oh, thank God," I whisper, the deck of business cards dropping from my hands and onto the floor. "You're here."

Damon's eyes travel from my shaking hands to Liam, and then back to me with a burning intensity.

"What the fuck did he do to you?" Damon asks. But before I can answer, he's stalking to the front door. "You're not welcome here," he says to Liam. "If I ever see you here again, I will use my bare hands to make sure you never spew that vitriol ever again."

"I'll pray for you, Brooks," Liam responds, his voice

sickly sweet. His gaze turns to me. “My offer still stands if you ever change your mind.” And then he walks off.

Damon grabs my arm and spins me around. “What fucking offer?”

I pull away and walk to the front desk, bending over to pick up the business cards that I dropped.

“He offered me a job. Told me he’d pay double what I get paid here.”

“Jesus,” Damon breathes, rubbing his face. “That motherfucker.”

“He really hates you guys,” I add, crooking a smile.

Damon’s eyes are black holes of unfeeling rage as his fists clench at his sides. “He has a good reason to.”

I busy myself with the cards again so that I can gather the courage to ask what I really want to know.

“Does it have anything to do with Silas’s parents?”

Damon doesn’t answer, so I look up at him as I mold the deck. He’s leaning against the opposite wall, chewing on his bottom lip. I wait, watching the way his chest still rises and falls quickly from his interaction with Liam.

“It’s not really my story to tell, Lennon. All I can say is that Liam is the reason Silas and his brother, Ledger, grew up the way that they did.” He pauses. “He got what he deserved.” He rubs his bottom lip with his thumb. “Honestly, he deserved worse.”

“What did you guys do?” I ask, setting the cards back in the card holder at the front of the desk.

“You should be asking Silas what *Liam* did.”

I swallow and look down. “He’s a creep.”

Damon nods and pushes up from the wall. "Stay away from him, Lennon."

I raise my brows and quirk a smile. "He said the same thing about you guys."

He stops in front of me and my breathing hitches. How is it possible that a person's eyes can be so dark, yet so alive all at once? They are two black pools into his soul, and they bore into mine effortlessly.

"Do you trust us, or do you trust him? We're not going to make you stay here. You're not beholden to this job."

My heart beats faster with each breath, and I swallow as I look into Damon's eyes. They're full of anger, but they're also warm. I've never had such a visceral reaction to any of them, like the one I did with Liam today. Even when Silas ordered me to clean the bathroom, even when they insulted me, I never felt unsafe with them. I never had that fight or flight response like I did with Liam.

"I trust you," I say quietly.

Something changes in Damon's eyes then, and I see the shift. The feral gaze that takes over as his eyes wander down to my lips.

"You shouldn't," he states, his voice hoarse.

"And why not?" I ask, intentionally poking the bear. Out of all of them, Damon seems the most unhinged to me. It's almost exciting to taunt him, thrilling to see how he'll react.

"Because up until a few days ago, we wanted to do bad things to you, Lennon."

I twist my lips to the side. "Like what? Scrub some toilets? It's going to take a lot more to–"

"No," he growls, shaking his head as he bares his teeth. "Not like scrubbing toilets." My blood turns cold at his words, at the *way* he says them. It's so animalistic. "And if Jude had his way, he'd probably still do those things if we let him."

I shake my head and shove him away. "It's been ten years, Damon." I turn to walk away, but he grabs me and pins me against the desk.

"Are you saying you wouldn't deserve it?" His breath is hot and heady, and it sends shivers down my spine as it tickles my face.

"What are you talking about?" I ask, breathing heavily.

"Graduation night," he answers, his voice low. His hand moves up to my jaw, a finger coming underneath my chin. "Are you saying we don't deserve to get vengeance for that night?"

"Silas said–"

He slowly shakes his head. "I'm not Silas."

I swallow as his calloused thumb caresses my skin, and my eyes flutter closed as a tremble works through me at the gesture. It's suddenly so hot in here–so hot, but also so cold...

His hand trails down my neck to my exposed chest, and my nipples betray me by peaking against the fabric of my unpadded sports bra. They rub against the fabric, and I have to stifle a moan as his finger does circles around one of them.

"Is this for me, princess?" he asks, his voice rough and grating. "Or are you just a little slut for anyone who gives you any attention?" I open my mouth to retort, but his other hand comes over my mouth. "Did that fiancé of yours not know how to properly fuck you?"

I look up at him with wide eyes. His hand is salty, and I yearn to flick my tongue out and taste it, but I don't. Instead, I take a step back as his hands fall to his sides.

"I'll ask you again. Do you trust us?"

I stare at him for a second too long before I turn and walk away without answering.

twenty-four

Lennon

That night, as I'm walking into work, I try not to think about how I can still imagine what Jude's come tasted like, or how my body reacted to Damon's breath as it tickled my skin. Neither of them is my type, and neither of them has *ever* been on my radar until recently. And then there's the fact that I am *way* more inexperienced than they all are. I mean, just look at the three of them. There's no way women aren't falling over themselves to sleep with them. All I have to my name is an incredible night in Cancun, once, with Wright. That was the only night he was able to make me come. I had to rely on my handy vibrators to get the job done all of those other times.

I shake the thought away and walk through the door of Savage Ink. Silas is sitting at the desk, brows furrowed as he scans something on the large computer. He doesn't look over as I set my purse down, and it's only when I clear my throat that he looks up at me. His cerulean eyes scan my face briefly before moving down my black skinny jeans, white tee, and heeled boots. They linger for a second on the boots, then he cocks his head and leans back as he gives me a lopsided grin.

"You copied my outfit," he observes, crossing his arms.

Indeed, we are matching–white shirts, black pants, black boots. Except he fills out his shirt way better than I do. And today, he has a rosary around his neck.

"What's that?" I ask, pointing to the string of beads.

He looks down and fingers the necklace. "Irony," he answers, his voice low.

He doesn't have to say anything else, and I don't inquire. Instead, I walk to the restroom to make sure it's tidy before clients begin to come in. When I come back out, Silas is standing near the front door, looking down at his phone.

"I'm running out for some drinks and food. Want anything?"

"I'll have whatever you're having."

He stares at me for a beat. "You don't have to do that around me, you know."

I shake my head. "Do what?"

He sighs, brushing his lip with his thumb and looking away for a second. "Be amenable." I tilt my head in confusion, and he huffs a laugh. "If you could have anything in the world right now, what would it be?"

I grin and answer without hesitating. “A cupcake.”

He smirks. “There we go. One cupcake to go. Any flavor preferences?”

I shrug. “Vanilla?”

He gives me a dark, lewd smile. “Not for long.”

And then he turns and walks out.

Not for long? What the hell does *that* mean? I’m still questioning it when I hear someone enter the studio. I turn to ask Silas what he meant by that, but Liam is standing against the door.

And two other guys flank him.

“Um,” I mumble, looking around. “Hi. Can I help you?”

Liam’s eyes narrow. “Last chance, Lennon. Come work for us and leave this place behind. We can show you things you never thought were possible. We can ensure your happiness. But you need to leave this place now. After tonight, my offer will no longer be valid.”

I cross my arms, thoroughly pissed that my last response wasn’t enough for him. “I am not interested in joining a fucking cult,” I say, raising my voice just a bit. My eyes flick to his two sidekicks. They’re older, like him, and though they seem to be putting on a nice front, they’re both standing against either side of the door, as if they’re not going to let me pass. My stomach drops at the realization that I can’t count on Silas to save me like Damon did yesterday, since I know he won’t be back right away. I can’t count on any of them... Damon and Jude aren’t even here. “What do you want from me?”

Liam looks at his sidekicks, and they turn to leave.

"I'm sorry that you're going to get mixed up in all of this, Lennon," he snarls quietly. "These guys are not good people."

"And you are?" I ask, raising my eyebrows.

He growls. "You're making a mistake."

"I'm fine, thank you," I snap.

He takes a step forward, but I stand my ground. Even as he stops a mere foot from me, I don't budge. I don't break eye contact. Isn't that what they say in the wilderness? If you break eye contact, that means you're submitting?

I open my mouth to ask him to leave, when someone pulls him away, making him stumble. He catches himself on one of the chairs, almost falling to the floor. I look at Damon, who is watching Liam with wrathful fury. His fists are up.

Liam is panting as he holds his hands up, surrendering. "I had to try one last time, Brooks."

Silas and Jude walk through the door a second later, and they glare at Liam as he walks out, giving me one last look before walking away.

"You okay?" Silas asks, setting a bag down on the desk.

"What the fuck did he want?" Jude asks.

I shrug, rubbing my neck. "I don't know." I can't quite shake the uneasiness of his threat, though.

I'm sorry that you're going to get mixed up in all of this, Lennon.

Silas reaches into his bag and brings me a plastic

container with six, full-sized funfetti cupcakes as Jude and Damon walk over to their stations.

"I said vanilla," I whine, and he smiles as he opens the container and pulls one out for me.

"And I said not for long," he repeats. "Do we look like vanilla to you?"

I snort. "Not exactly." I take the cupcake and peel the paper off. "Why is Liam trying to recruit me?" Out of the three of them, he will know best.

Silas sighs, and I notice Damon and Jude turning to face us as he shakes his head.

"He suspects we're behind the recent attack on his members," he answers, crossing his arms, and I don't like the way his lips quirk upwards. "Several people in his church have been turning up with face tattoos," he adds.

Realization hits me. "You–you're–" I look at his rosary. "You wear that to taunt him."

Silas shakes his head, and his golden hair falls in front of his beautiful face. "I wear it to show him that he didn't win."

I smirk. "It's like the modern-day version of the Scarlet Letter."

He shrugs and looks down at his feet. "My parents got wrapped up in their bullshit. Church of the Rapture. That's their name."

It sends chills down my spine. "Rapture?"

"Liam and his fellow cult members think the apocalypse will come soon, and all Believers–dead or alive–will ascend to the clouds to meet Jesus," Jude summarizes, his voice droll. "They're a bunch of homophobic, racist idiots."

My eyebrows shoot up as I look back at Silas. "And your parents..."

His eyes find mine. "They believed him. Gave him a ton of money to continue spreading the gospel. He was manipulating them." He pauses, opening and closing his mouth a couple of times. "They're unwell now. Hospitalized."

I let out a heavy sigh, feeling like there is more to that story. "Wow. I'm so sorry."

He shrugs again. "Each day away from that fucking cult is a victory. I'm getting my revenge. Slowly, but surely."

I nod. "So, that's why he's after you. Because you're outing them by inking their faces."

He smiles. "Among other things. We have the capacity to do something about it. Why wouldn't we?"

"Scarlet Letter Vigilantes," I add, twisting my lips to the side.

"Can I get business cards with that name?" Damon asks from his place at his station.

I smirk, and then Damon and Jude busy themselves with their prep. I turn to Silas, but before I can speak, he takes a step closer to me.

"How's it healing?" he asks, his voice low, just for me to hear. "May I?" he adds, reaching out for my shirt.

I nod, and he takes another step forward, unbuttoning my pants and tugging them down ever so slightly. I try not to audibly gasp as his calloused fingers graze my skin. He lowers my underwear and takes a quick peek at my healing tattoo. I've been keeping it covered with underwear, so it doesn't rub against the rough texture of my jeans. Silas runs a finger over the sensitive area, and the sensation makes me shiver.

"It looks good," he murmurs, pulling my underwear and pants back up. I button them as my eyes find his. His icy blue irises are darker somehow, and his lids are hooded. Licking his lips, he takes a step back. "Have you been taking care of it?"

I give him a small smile. My heart is hammering inside of my chest. "Yes. I am taking very good care of it, master," I respond in a teasing tone, in an attempt to alleviate this growing tension.

I doesn't work, though.

His eyes darken further, and their intensity bores into me, causing me to start breathing heavier as my pulse whooshes in my ears.

"Don't call me that," he commands.

I cock my head to the side in confusion. "What, *master*?" He makes a low humming sound in his throat, and I swallow. "I was joking–"

"Don't make me show you how much that word *isn't* a joke, Lennon," he adds, raising his eyebrows as he saunters off.

What.

The.

Hell.

twenty-five

Lennon

My eyes are burning by the time I wrap up for the evening. I didn't realize how crappy I slept last night, and how tired I am right now because of it. Tonight passes by uneventfully, with no more signs of Liam or anything else amiss. And the guys didn't have me scrubbing toilets tonight, either. Their revenge plot seems to have petered out, and I'm not quite sure why. Something about my mom insulting me, or about the tattoo, seems to have softened them a bit. And then everything with Liam...

The tattoo is a reminder for you. Not for us. For you.

That maybe all along, we were the good guys.

That maybe you fit in here–at Savage.

With us.

My throat constricts when I think of Silas' words, about how different they are from the first encounter we had the night I moved in. I glance at them as they clean up their stations, and a warm feeling spreads throughout my body as I watch them bicker with each other. I didn't expect to like them, to like working here, or being their friend. But I do, and somehow, I feel more like myself here than I ever have.

My phone dings loudly from my purse, and I glance down at the screen. I gasp and my mouth opens and closes as I read Lola's words.

Just found out there's a condo in my complex that will be vacant soon. I signed you up to view it tomorrow morning at 11. Hope you don't mind. :)

"Why do you look like you just won the lottery?" Jude asks as he walks up to me and begins wiping down the front desk.

"Because Lola just got me in to see a condo in her complex tomorrow morning." I grin as I look up at him—at all of them. "If it goes well, I won't have to live upstairs anymore."

I expect him to smile, but instead he just clenches his jaw and looks back at Silas and Damon. Before I can ask about their strange reactions, my phone dings again, and Lola offers to pick me up in the morning. I quickly respond, and by the time I look up again, Jude is nowhere to be found.

"You're going to need furniture," Silas says, his voice gritting out roughly.

I purse my lips to the side and lean back. "It's too bad I didn't bring my things from Manhattan. I was in such a rush to leave..." I trail off.

Damon leans against one of the mirrors. "You still have stuff at that prick's house?"

I nod. "I only brought the basics. No furniture, since that was all the designer's style, not mine. But I do have some things there. I always envisioned going back, but honestly... the thought of running into Wright terrifies me."

Damon and Silas share a look, and I frown. "What?" They look at me and then pretend to busy themselves with the antibacterial wipes. "Don't play dumb. Jude acted weird, too. What is it?"

Silas sighs. "We should go back and get your shit."

I bite my lower lip and cross my arms. "I still have a key."

Damon smirks. "We should go tonight."

I huff a laugh. "It's two in the morning," I whine. "Manhattan is over four hours away." I know, because I took a filthy bus from Manhattan to Boston, and a taxi to Greythorn. "I'm also exhausted."

Jude wanders into the studio from the bathroom, drying his hands on a paper towel.

"What did I miss?" he asks, looking between the three of us.

"I think we're going to New York tonight," Silas responds, his eyes finding mine. They *burn* through me, pinning me to the spot.

I shake my head. "No. We can find another night, but–"

"There is no other night, Lennon," Damon says matter-of-factly. "We're here almost every night, and on our night off, we usually have our thing at the house."

It's then that I realize they need that night, need the art, and the way they can bleed creativity. I can hear the desperation in Damon's voice–the longing. I look at all three of them.

They're artists who will starve without an outlet.

"Okay," I concede. "But I'm not driving."

Jude grabs his jacket and grins. "I never sleep, so I'll drive us."

I stand up and grab my purse. "Which one of you has a car?" I ask, realizing later how stupid the question is. They all just laugh, and I'm left with burning cheeks. I stifle a yawn as I use the restroom quickly.

Pulling an all-nighter is something I haven't done since college. I never went out with Wright, and if we did, we left early. He insisted it was because he had to be up early for work, but he always had an excuse–even on weekends. I'm starting to realize he was the antithesis to fun. I finish up in the bathroom, splashing my face with cold water and patting it dry before exiting the bathroom.

When I walk into the studio, all three guys are waiting for me by the front door.

"Wouldn't you all rather be sleeping?" I tease.

"We don't sleep, princess," Silas answers, holding the door open for me. I ignore the way his arm brushes mine, and the way my whole body explodes with tingles as his hand finds my lower back. We walk to a white SUV, and I stop in front of it.

"Whose car is this?" I ask, glancing at the tinted windows warily.

"Mine," Jude answers.

"Shotgun," Silas calls, jogging to the passenger side.

I shoot him an evil stare, and then I glance up at Damon, who looks about ready to devour me whole.

"Four hours in the backseat with me?" he asks, smiling monstrously. "That'll be fun."

I fall asleep instantly, especially since Jude plays his psycho killer classical music playlist. I smile as I drift off, somehow feeling like I've perhaps found a group of people that cares enough about me to drive through the night, and over eight hours round trip, just to ensure I have all my things in my new place. The thought is so unfamiliar to me. I only ever had Mindy and Wright to count on, and even then, the latter turned out not to be so reliable. So the fact that these guys–guys I've known almost my whole life, but whom I thought hated me–are giving up their sleep, for me... it almost feels unfathomable.

It isn't until we enter Manhattan four and a half hours later that I wake up, the stop and go traffic jerking the car enough to rouse me. I sit up, realizing with horror that I've drooled all over Damon's shoulder. He just chuckles and hands me a tissue, but I slap it out of his hand and wipe my mouth with the back of my hand.

"Morning, princess," he mutters.

"Did I sleep the entire way?" I ask incredulously.

He tilts his head and scoots a bit closer. "If your snoring was any indication..." I groan, covering my face. He wraps an arm around my shoulder and leans in until his mouth is over my ear. "Don't be embarrassed. You're incredibly sexy when you sleep, snoring or no snoring."

My cheeks heat, and I smile. "I find that hard to believe."

I glance up front, and Silas is fast asleep in the passenger seat. Jude is staring straight ahead, a pair of aviator glasses perched on the bridge of his nose. The sun is high now, above the buildings, blasting the car with shiny light. I sigh contentedly. I *love* New York. And I especially love New York in the morning. Summer mornings, before it gets too hot, are perfect. Before the tourists get bussed in, before the shops open, when it's just the locals out for a coffee run, or the occasional walk of shamer. I smile as I look out of my window, watching the brownstones as we pass them. A deep, gnawing sort of ache starts in my chest. This was my home for the last six years. A part of my soul is embedded into this city, even if I know deep down that it's not for me. It was still more of a home to me than Greythorn ever was.

"You miss it," Damon observes, his voice low as his hand comes to rest on my thigh.

I stiffen at his touch and nod. "I do."

He's quiet as I watch the city pass me by, as I remember the place I left behind.

"Are you nervous?" he asks, his fingers trailing up my thigh.

I turn to face him and quirk an eyebrow. "You're distracting me."

He grins a wide, beautiful grin. His wild hair and dark eyes cause my stomach to bottom out, and then he licks his lips.

"Sorry, I've just spent the last four hours staring at you while you sleep. I'm feeling a bit cooped up. Wild. *Feral.*"

I swallow thickly, a shockwave of hot electricity running down my limbs, pooling in my throbbing clit. I should balk at his words. He was just *watching* me sleep? Why? It sounds creepy, but as his eyes find mine, he shifts his body slightly so that he has better access to me.

"No," I whisper, looking up front.

"Don't stop on my account," Jude says, smirking at me in the rearview mirror. He doesn't say anything else, just turns the music up. It drowns out my conversation with Damon.

"You're all pigs," I chastise, pulling away from Damon against my body's will.

"Lennon," Damon growls. "Do you want me to stop pursuing you?"

I open and close my mouth several times. "I–you–you're pursuing me?"

He chuckles, his tenor deep. "Something like that." His hand roves up farther, to the apex of my thighs. To my horror, my legs spring apart, allowing him to do exactly what he wants. Leaning closer, so that Jude doesn't hear, he begins whispering into my ear.

"Do you like that my hand is resting on your wet little cunt, princess?"

I gasp, but his other hand comes over my mouth. I glance at Jude in the rearview mirror, but he's either pretending not to hear us, or he's distracted by the large intersection we're about to enter.

"Tell me what you want, Lennon," he whispers again, his fingers pressing into my clit, clawing at it, cupping it roughly. I buck my hips against his palm, the sensation causing shivers to run all the way down to my toes. "Good girl," he mutters, his fingers brushing the spot I need it most.

"I don't know what I want," I respond, resisting the urge to grind myself into his touch.

He cups me harder, his hand circling the spot that's now wet through my jeans.

"Your pussy is lying, then," he growls.

"Do we have to do it here?" I hiss, trying to push his hand away.

"Not an exhibitionist?" he muses, smiling as he flicks my clit. I inhale sharply, the pain surprising yet welcome.

"No," I breathe. I'm nearly panting now.

"Do you touch yourself, Lennon?" he asks, his breath hot on my ear. "Do you know what feels good?" I nod. He purrs in response. "Good. Show me what you do." I open my mouth to protest, but his free hand cups my lips again. "Be quiet," he whispers. "And show me."

He removes both hands and leans back, crossing his arms. My eyes zero in on the large bulge in his pants, and he cocks his head and smiles.

"We'll deal with that later. Now. Touch yourself."

I sneak another peek at Jude and Silas. One is still asleep, and the other is busy with the directions, since driving in Manhattan is not for the faint of heart. I swallow and look at Damon again. He's not going to relent, not going to let me win this one. I can tell by the way his intense gaze hasn't left my face, how his pulse thrums in his neck, and how he's trying to calm his rapid breathing.

I reach down and unbutton my pants. The shock and mortification of what I'm about to do flames my cheeks, but Damon's heated gaze is tracking every movement, every inch of my wandering hands. He leans back a bit more, and I hope to God that Jude can't see below our waists. Damon rubs the bulge in his pants–his hand practiced, familiar. The thought is enough for me to unzip my black pants and thrust my hips forward as I scoot down in the seat.

I close my eyes as I begin to work my fingers around my clit. Damon is right, I'm completely soaked. My entire core is throbbing, and it gets worse when I see Damon unzip his pants. My eyes bulge out of my head when he whips out his monster cock. It's huge, and when I meet his gaze again, something profound moves behind his eyes as he begins to stroke the thick, veiny shaft. I glance once again to the front, but thanks to the noise and our positions, Silas and Jude aren't able to see what we're doing.

Unless they turn around.

The thought sends a fiery blast through me, and I bite my lower lip as my fingers move into my underwear.

"Let me taste you," Damon demands, nodding to my hand.

"W–what?" I ask, my voice strained.

"Give me your finger."

I hesitate for a moment, and Damon then takes it upon himself to reach for my hand and pull it to his mouth. His tongue grazes the two fingers that had been sliding between my folds, and he closes his eyes and growls. It's a sound so low, I feel it rather than hear it. His tongue swirls around my flesh, and I buck my hips as it flicks between my two fingers.

Oh, what we could do with that tongue...

He drops my hand. "Keep going."

I use the wetness from his mouth and continue, not realizing how much I need this release. How *wound up* I really am. The bundle of nerves at the apex of my thighs ignites, and I speed up my tempo. To my horror, I can *hear* how wet I am, and I nearly stop–until Damon begins to jerk himself faster, panting quietly.

I watch him as he strokes his cock, how his hand grips it firmly, how his fist rotates slightly when he gets to the head. The head that's wet with precum.

Because of me.

I spread my legs wider, and I can feel the flush working its way up my chest, neck, and eventually, my face. I don't even know what's happening. Why am I doing this? It's the craziest thing I've ever done, I think. I move my hand faster, keeping my lower lip between my teeth as I work myself higher.

I thought I'd be embarrassed, but in the moment, this doesn't feel embarrassing.

It feels perverse, and wrong, but *so, so* good.

"Use your other hand to fuck yourself," he commands.

I don't hesitate this time. I quickly look out of the window, and I can tell we're only a few blocks away now. We have five minutes at most, and I'm determined to finish.

Using my other hand, I insert two fingers and buck my hips against my hand. I'm nearly gasping for air now, though I try to keep myself quiet as wave after wave of pleasure unleashes inside of me. Damon is massaging his balls with his other hand, and every movement causes him to jerk as he watches me. Precum is dripping down his palm, and his forehead has a thin sheen of sweat.

God, this is so fucking hot.

We're both frantic now. Close to climaxing, almost out of time... I can see the feverish need explode on Damon's face.

"You first," he growls. "Come for me, Lennon."

My body is hot, and every part of my skin is tingling with pleasure. His words snap something inside of me, and every muscle that had been tense now releases. A wave of heat explodes in my core, sending a smattering of electricity down my limbs. My toes curl in my boots as the orgasm slams through me, and it takes everything not to scream, not to holler Damon's name.

"Holy fuck," I whisper, my climax cleaving through me. I'm positively fucking my hand now, my hips working in undulating motions as the last of it leaves my jerking body.

Shuddering, I let out a long sigh. I look over at Damon, but before I can say anything, he reaches over and grabs my hair, pulling my face onto his cock.

"Swallow," he instructs, his voice hoarse, but he doesn't force me. I look up at him and smile before bending down, taking his thick shaft into my mouth.

It's warm, and his skin is taut over his throbbing erection. I move up and down his cock, and he bucks his hips against me. His hand grips my hair tighter, and I can tell by the way I feel his shaft bobbing between my lips that he's about to come. Reaching over, I cup his balls as the first spurt hits my tongue, his cock pulsing through his release. I squeeze my eyes shut, letting him empty himself into the back of my throat. I swallow in quick succession, waiting for him to finish, and then I remove my mouth and sit up.

I grin as my face takes in his expression–shocked, bemused, fervent. He smiles back as I zip and button my pants, and nearly ten seconds later, we pull up in front of my old apartment building.

"Ready, princess?" Damon asks, closing his pants too.

I shake my head. "No."

And it's true. Despite the fun we just had, nothing will prepare me for what's about to go down.

twenty-six

Jude

Damon must think I'm the world's biggest fucking idiot.

I try not to chuckle as we miraculously find parking a few blocks away, piling out of my car in one large exodus. I know when he's craving some pussy, and I know what his eyes look like when he's about to fuck. A quick glance into the back seat confirmed what I already knew, and now I had to figure out a way to hide my raging hard-on. I frown as I lock the car, and we walk up Park Avenue, turning left until we hit the park.

It's a little past seven in the morning, and the over-achieving runners are out. There are also a few frazzled families out for coffee, toddlers in tow, with the parents looking utterly exhausted. Lennon leads us down 73rd Street, and just as we see Central Park across the street, she turns to the looming building to our left. We follow her onto Fifth Avenue, and several feet away is a green awning. I look at the guys, and Silas just furrows his brows. Lennon seems a bit off kilter–we have Damon to thank for that, I suppose–so I grab her elbow and pull her back just as we reach the awning.

"Shouldn't we have a plan in place?" I ask, nodding to the building.

She sighs. "He's not here."

I narrow my eyes. "How do you know?"

She reaches into her purse and unlocks her phone, showing me a random map with a blue dot in the middle.

"We used to share our locations with each other. He must've forgotten to switch it off. He's somewhere in Brooklyn, probably with that red-headed b–" She composes herself, her spine straight as she clears her throat. "Anyway, he's not here."

"What about the doorman?" Silas asks, running a hand through his hair. He looks like he just woke up, sporting bloodshot eyes and rumpled hair.

"Earl will let us in," she states matter-of-factly. "And if not, I have a key. Please just trust me."

I haven't had the courage to look at Damon yet, so I glance back at Lennon. In this area of Manhattan, we look out of place. We've already gotten a few dirty looks, and I don't need anyone to foil our plan before we get inside.

"Then let's go up," I suggest. "Get off the street." I make eye contact with a middle-aged woman in yoga pants. She watches us warily, so I smirk and wink. That causes her to scurry away in fear. I stifle a laugh.

Silas follows her through the revolving doors. Damon claps me on the back, and the motion causes me to jump.

"Like what you saw in the car?" he asks, his lips inches from my ear.

"You're a dumbass," I chide, frowning.

"You didn't answer my question, Vanderbilt."

"Fuck off, Damon." I throw his arm off my back, and all I hear is his low, rumbling chuckle in response.

twenty-seven

Lennon

Despite my racing heart, I'm able to get my emotions in check in the three seconds it takes to walk through the shiny gold revolving doors. The distanced familiarity is strange. It's been over three weeks since I've been here, yet it feels like months. *Years even.* Earl has his feet propped up on the front desk like usual, and when he realizes it's me, he jumps up and grins. Even now, his benign middle-aged-ness brings me comfort. My father was never really around, but Earl was always someone I could count on when I moved in here.

"Tell me it's not my favorite occupant and her–" He glances behind me, eyebrows arching when he takes in the guys. "Your friends?" he asks, his voice prim and polite, though I can hear the frenzied question on his tongue.

"Hi, Earl," I say smoothly, smiling as we hug. "These are some friends from high school." I swallow, ready to tell him the entire story. It had been the other guy–the one who was always on his phone–the night I stormed out of here. I wonder what Wright has told him, if anything? "Unfortunately, I'm just here to pick up some things." I pause, and I can sense the guys behind me waiting patiently. "Truth be told, Earl... Wright cheated on me, and I won't be back. I had to move back home to Massachusetts."

He whistles, shaking his head. "Is it that red-headed woman–"

I wince, squeezing my eyes shut. It still hurts too damn much to think about her stupid face.

"Yep. That's her. She's his assistant."

Earl smirks. "You were always too good for him, Len."

I hear one of the guys shift his weight behind me, and my cheeks heat at Earl's kind words.

"Well, thank you." I walk to the elevator. "We won't be long."

Earl shrugs as he resumes his position behind the desk. "Doesn't matter to me. Take all the time you need, sweetheart." He winks as he raises his feet up onto the desk again, flipping the newspaper out in his lap. "If you leave a few holes in the walls, I promise not to tattle."

I grin and look behind me. Silas, Damon, and Jude are all looking around the lobby. I suppose to an outsider, this place feels luxurious. Classic Upper East Side, with lots of new money accents, marble, and gold. I liked it when I lived here, but I'd never lived anywhere but a place like this, so it felt like home from the very first day. Wright was quite choosy, and this place fit his long list of requirements, which said a lot.

I motion for the guys to follow me as I walk into the elevator. Then I give Earl one last wave before we all climb in, and once the doors shut, Damon clears his throat.

"Spit it out," I growl, turning to face him.

He wiggles his eyebrows, his tongue rolling around the inside of his cheek, and the double entendre slams through me.

Spit it out...

I huff a laugh and shake my head. Just as I'm about to call him a pervert, Jude reaches out and gestures to the floors.

"I'm assuming we're going up to 'P'?" he asks, his voice smooth and teasing.

"Yep. I have a key card." I reach into my purse and pull out the black card I was always so accustomed to carrying around. I tap it against the black box, and it beeps. Right now, in here with them, this whole process just feels pretentious and unnecessary.

"How long did you live here?" Silas asks, crossing his arms and leaning against the mirrored wall as we head up to the top floor. Damon and Silas are wearing white shirts, like me, and their ink mirrored all around the elevator shaft is exquisite. Jude is in a black Henley, and I didn't realize before, but he's wearing a small cross around his neck.

Another taunt for Liam, I'm sure.

"About three years," I say wistfully. "After college, Wright and I moved to the city. As you can probably guess, we lived in this area and knew we wanted to buy an apartment in one of these buildings. One of Wright's clients–Wright is an attorney, by the way–told him about this place before it went on the market, so we made a cash offer, and..." I trail off, my chest flushing. I sound like such a snob.

The elevator dings, and the doors open to the place I considered my first real home. My eyes sting as I walk in, setting my purse down on the marble entryway table and kicking my shoes off, out of habit. *God, I used to just wait for Martha to clean up after me,* I think, referring to our housekeeper. Silas, Damon, and Jude follow suit, taking their shoes off before they each wander around, eyebrows raised.

"Damn," Jude murmurs, running a finger over the pristine, white marble of the kitchen. "Your current place is a hovel compared to this."

He's not wrong.

Tall, domed ceilings encompass the space, with hardwood floors throughout. And plush Persian rugs along with gorgeous, matching furniture decorate each room. I walk through the foyer and into the formal sitting room, my eyes looking over everything with a fresh set of eyes. The art we hung on the walls, the fabric I picked out for the throw pillows, the candles I bought at the boutique in the Village... I loved it here once, but now that I've had some time away–some time to think–I realize just how *much* it all is.

The whole first floor is open concept, so my eyes wander over to the large chef's kitchen with modern stainless-steel appliances. The white marble on the counters is the most exclusive type of marble, and we waited nearly three months for it to come in from Italy. I run my hands over a thick, black vein in the marble, and a lump forms in my throat. Pretentious or not, this was my home. My name may not have been on the deed, but I lived here, loved here, made love here, cooked and baked here, grew up here...

"Hey," Silas says gently, his hand coming to the small of my back. "Let's get your things and go."

I nod. "Yeah. I know. It's just... now that I'm here, I don't really want anything, you know?"

He quirks his lips to the side, and his blue eyes pin me to the spot. "You sure?" He tilts his chin to the other side of the kitchen, and I follow his gaze. "Not even that?"

My stomach lurches when I see my copper stand mixer. "Oh my God," I whisper, turning back to Silas. "You're right. That is a special edition, professional-grade stand mixer." I walk over to it, smiling. "I'll go get a box."

I end up taking most of my things. I'm quite petty about it, too. If I bought it with my own money, or it was gifted to me–such as my jewelry–I take it. We end up using seven large boxes that barely fit in the trunk of Jude's

SUV. Silas helps me go through my things, and Damon does the heavy lifting. I have no idea what Jude does for an entire hour, but I catch him wandering around and touching things randomly. I make one more trip up alone, wandering around the penthouse and saying a proper goodbye. I cry for a few minutes, sitting on the couch I spent days picking out online, and then I stand up, brush my shirt off, and walk out.

Lucky for me, Silas has given up the passenger seat, so I climb inside. Jude turns on his serial killer music, and within a few minutes, I pass out from exhaustion once again.

twenty-eight

Silas

We get back to Greythorn with half an hour to spare for Lennon's condo viewing. The thought of her living alone, not living above Savage, makes my stomach sour. I like having her close, and I like knowing she's safe. She doesn't need to know that after the first night, back when I swore I hated her, I turned our front door camera to face her front door instead. If anyone attempts to get to her, I will know about it with an alarm on my phone.

Maybe it's possessive, or maybe it's just smart. She's alone up there, and though Greythorn is usually safe, there is a growing list of people in this town that I don't fucking trust.

We drop her off at her apartment and I offer to grab my car and pick her up so we can drive to the condo. That's the other issue. This place is on the outskirts of town, a solid eight-minute drive or forty-minute walk. Lennon doesn't have a car, and I don't like the idea of her walking down single-lane roads by herself. She'd need a car as soon as possible, but knowing her, she will insist on walking everywhere to save on cash.

I know she'll get suspicious if I start throwing even more money at her...

She's hesitant to put down roots. Especially in the town that did her so dirty growing up. She resents Greythorn, and buying a car would be one more step in solidifying her suburb lifestyle. Like us, she hates the suburbs. I know it goes against everything we all stand for. I *know* the longing she feels, the way the city makes her come alive. I know, because I'm the exact same way.

Which is why the guys and I have been talking about her moving in with us.

It's quick, but it makes the most sense. I even have a spare car she can use. It's not like my parents will be in any shape to drive anytime soon. We work together, and the house is big enough for her to feel like she has her own space. She wouldn't need to pay me rent just yet, and she could decide whether or not she wants to stay in Greythorn without committing to a year-long lease.

I'm distractedly waiting outside of the shop in my car when Lennon hops into the passenger seat.

"Nice car," she purrs, running her hand over the black leather seat.

She buckles herself in, and I let my eyes trail down her bare legs. She's changed into a black tank top and black leather pleated skirt. She's also wearing white converse, which makes my cock stir inside my pants. *Something about a woman wearing a skirt and converse...* It all accentuates her legs, which are golden and toned, with just enough flesh to grab onto. I shift in my seat to conceal my ever-growing erection.

"Thanks. It was a consolation prize for moving back to this dump." I tap the steering wheel of my Porsche.

She tilts her head and turns to face me. "You hate it here," she states. "Why stay?"

I shrug. "My parents were unwell, as you know. I had to get their estate in order, and I plan to list the house next year. I opened a shop here because we always talked about expanding, and the place–your mom's building–is reasonably priced."

"Who's running the shop in Boston?" she asks, picking at her nails.

"Our apprentices. They worked under us for a year, and when I decided to move here, I didn't expect Damon and Jude to follow me."

"You guys are quite attached at the hip," she jokes, and she has no idea just how right she is.

"It was always supposed to be a temporary move. Boston is where we love to be. We don't need to have our parties there. We get fulfillment just by being around other creatives. It was only when we moved here that we felt... suffocated."

She's quiet for a few minutes. "Greythorn is nice, but I know what you mean. I'm shocked I made it out alive all those years ago."

I smirk, reaching over and placing a hand on her bare

knee. I love the sound that gets caught in her throat, and the sharp inhale when my skin makes contact with hers.

"Didn't I tell you that you're one of us? I should just start having you apprentice under me," I add, the notion exciting me in more ways than one.

She makes a face and shakes her head. "I'm not good with needles. Besides, I want to open my own bakery one day." The second the words are out, I can see the shock on her face. "I've never actually told anyone that before." She turns to face me. "Not even Wright."

I grip the steering wheel a bit harder with my free hand as her words sink in. "You should."

She scoffs. "It's not that easy." When I sneak a peek at her, she's looking out the window. I can see the wheels turning. I remove my hand from her knee because I know it's distracting her, and I want to hear this. "It takes money, some sort of nest egg to buy everything I would need. Second, I'd need a space, and third, I'd need to be able to prove I could sustain the business. I'd need a solid business plan, otherwise I'd just be throwing money away."

"That's true. But there's also the part about taking a chance before it's too late."

She turns to face me. "What do you mean?"

I smile. "I'm not saying you shouldn't do all of that." I turn into the condo complex and park. Turning to face her, I tilt my head. "I don't think you need to wait until everything is perfect. Sometimes you need to make the leap *despite* having all of your ducks in a row. You have a good product, yes?"

Her eyes widen. "Um–yes," she answers.

I nod. "Okay. People love bakeries. Once you have the money to open up shop, I think you should try."

She just stares at me. "That's easy for you to say."

"Oh?" I love the little smile she's giving me.

"Yeah. Did you not have your parents' money to start up Ignite in Boston?"

I scoff. "I've never had access to a cent of their money, Lennon."

This must surprise her, because she rears her head back. "Really?"

I shake my head. "Nope. Never. After... that summer..." I say slowly, rubbing my lower lip with my thumb, "we moved out to Boston in the fall. Began building a savings. Had a shitty shop on the outskirts of town, then worked our way up. Every year, we would move. No one would lease to us because we didn't have credit." I look down, taking a deep breath as I think back to those years–the years we grew Ignite into what it is today. "One day, a famous quarterback tweeted about our work, and that was it. We blew up overnight. And we've been slammed solid ever since." I poke her arm, and she jumps. "Because we have a *solid product.*"

She smirks. "I just assumed..." She trails her hand over the leather seat again.

"That I bought this car with my parents' money?" She nods, and I grin. "No, princess. This was all me. All *us.* We worked hard as fuck for what we have. I mean, sure, we do live in their house. So that offsets living expenses. But everything else is all us, baby."

Her cheeks redden, and she looks around. “Impressive.”

I open the door and climb out. When I open her door for her, helping her out, she looks surprised again, so I change the subject.

“Ready to go view this dump?”

Her resounding laugh is the best sound in the world.

twenty-nine

Lennon

Silas and I arrive at a minute past eleven, and I follow the leasing agent's instructions to the large condo complex. I didn't realize how far I'd be from Savage, from everything, really. Even groceries would be a hassle with the closest store over a mile away...

I stand up straight and ignore the way Silas's eyebrows raise as his hand roves over the rusty door handle of the building. He kicks an old can of soda out of his way as we climb the carpeted stairs.

"I don't know if anyone's cleaned these stairs... ever," he mumbles. "At least Lola's side of the building is nicer than this."

I spin around. "I really don't need your input, but thanks."

He chuckles behind me, and I feel the fury begin to

heat my blood. "What other choice do I have?" I ask incredulously, my voice a little more shrill that I would've liked. "I need to get out of my mom's building. I have almost no money to my name, and this is the only affordable option in this godforsaken town–"

"Relax," he says gently, patting my ass. I swat his hand away. "I was mostly kidding. Let's go check it out, okay?"

I tromp up the rest of the stairs to the fourth story. No elevator. That's fine. I'll just figure out a grocery delivery service or something. I ignore the warning bells going off in my mind as we make our way past a few of the other doors. A couple of people are hanging out smoking cigarettes, and there's a baby crying somewhere. There is a leasing sign out front of the vacant condo, and the door is unlocked as I push it open.

"Oh, hi!" A woman is leaning against the counter on her phone, and she looks surprised to see me. "Do you have an appointment?"

I nod. "Yep. Lennon Rose. I have an appointment at eleven..." I look at my phone. "Sorry, we're a few minutes late." I glance at Silas out of the corner of my eye, but he's busy looking around the place with a disapproving scowl.

"Oh, Ms. Rose, I'm so sorry. I thought you'd cancelled, so I already approved the application we received from someone else this morning. I'm afraid the place has been rented. I'm just waiting for them to come back and sign the lease."

"Oh," I respond lightly, the ever-present lump in my

throat growing by the second. "That's fine. It's a little far from my job, anyway." Her words sink in slowly as I start to turn to leave. "Wait, I never cancelled my appointment."

She looks at Silas uncomfortably and shrugs. "Sorry. It was a man. He said he was calling on your behalf–"

"Let's go," Silas orders, dragging me back through the front door.

"Wait," I yell, pulling away from him as we get a few feet from the door. "Did you call her? Did you cancel my appointment?" My voice breaks on the last word. A few faces appear in the windows on this floor, looking to see what all the commotion is about, I'm sure.

Silas sighs, rubbing his face with his hands. "Jude called when we were in Manhattan and left a message."

The smoldering fury I felt before erupts into a full-body rage. "Why did you even drive me here if you knew the appointment had been cancelled?"

He tilts his head. "Because I wanted you to see first-hand how much of a bad decision it would be to move here."

I bite my tongue and close my eyes, my hands turning to fists at my sides. "I really hope you all have a good explanation for this–"

"Move in with us," he states simply, giving me his best shit-eating grin.

I explode, storming forward and shoving my hands against his chest. He stumbles back a bit, catching my hands at his chest and holding them there as I try my hardest to get my rage out.

We're both pressed against the side of the building now, and I'm sure the uneven concrete wall is digging into his skin.

Good.

I am burning. I want him to feel it. Why did they have to meddle? Why would they ever think I'd want to live with them? My breathing turns ragged as my words turn bitter and cold.

"Fuck you, Silas." My voice breaks on a sob. He's still clutching my hands at his chest, and everything, *everything*, from the last month comes crashing down onto me.

I'm back in my hometown, trying to rent a dingy apartment building, with a man who used to hate everything about me...

How did I get here?

I start to cry a bit harder, a guttural sound coming from me. My chest heaves as Silas's grip on my hands tightens.

"Move in with us, Lennon. It makes sense. We all work together, and you won't have to pay rent–"

I scream at that, shoving him hard as hot tears spring free from my eyes.

"I'm not your charity case," I growl, my lower lip wobbling. He furrows his brows and lets my hands go, but instead of pummeling him, I drop them to my side as I'm wracked with more sobs. "For some reason, you're always saving me, and I don't know why."

"Did you ever stop to consider the fact that we actually like you now? Back then, you were this perfect little princess, with your perfect little life–"

"My life was never perfect. My parents *hated* me. They wanted nothing to do with me, and I raised myself." I cut him off, twisting around as I walk down the stairs. I'm seeing red, and the tears are blurring my vision. Silas grabs my hand and presses my body into the wall of the stairwell. I yelp out loud as his face comes within inches of mine.

"It makes sense now, Lennon," he says calmly. "When we saw your mom that night–"

"Do you understand now why I need out of that place?" I ask, my voice hiccupping. "I don't–I don't want *anything* to do with her," I seethe, and before I know it, his hands are wrapping around my body tightly.

"I know," he murmurs, stroking the back of my head, which makes me cry even harder. "And I know what happened with that piece of shit fiancé, too. So please, let us *help* you. I will charge you rent if it makes you feel better. But I know your soul died the instant you came back here," he says carefully, his tone soft. "I don't want to see the fire inside of you go out forever because you got stuck here. This way, you can leave whenever you want. No lease contracts. No obligations. Just crashing with friends," he adds, squeezing me tighter.

God, my chest aches. More tears stream from my eyes, and I realize I'm not sad or angry anymore. This is a whole new emotion–something akin to what I imagine families feel. Warmth, compassion... *love.*

Something I've never had before.

"My soul didn't die when I came here," I explain, sniffling.

He pulls away, wiping the tears from my cheeks. "Yes, it did."

"How can you tell?" I ask, missing the way his body felt against mine.

"Because mine did, too. Like calls to like." I look up into his face, his crystal blue eyes boring into mine as something electric passes through my body. "You and I didn't grow up that different, you know. My parents were MIA, and I had to raise my brother by myself. It's too bad we weren't friends back then."

Friends *back then.*

As if he's insinuating we're friends now, which I guess we are. It's still hard for me to accept that people want to be my friend.

Especially after the way I used to act at Ravenwood Academy.

"I was too busy making your life miserable," I say glumly, keeping my eyes on him as I get the courage to finally speak the words I've wanted to for so long. "I'm sorry... for everything," I add, pausing as I look down at my feet. "I don't think I've ever formally apologized." When I look back up at Silas, he's frowning, but the look in his eyes isn't one of sadness.

He huffs a laugh and looks away, rubbing his lips with his hand.

"What?" I ask, feeling my lips tug into a smile. "I was so angry at you for so long, and then you go and cry in front of me and apologize, and all I can think about is how I want to kiss you."

I open my mouth to respond, but before a sound comes out, he presses me against the wall of the stairwell as his lips crash into mine. Heat flares through my body. His tongue flicks against mine sensually, and I can feel his erratic heartbeat thumping in his chest. His low moan makes me fist his shirt, makes me pull him closer. I *need* to feel what I do to him.

He reaches down and pins my hands behind me, gripping my waist with his free hand, taking control. My core clenches, and my clit swells as I feel his hard shaft against the waistband of my skirt. I whimper when his tongue parts my lips again. I reach for his belt buckle instinctively, not caring if we're in the stairwell of an apartment building.

Not caring if anyone sees us.

He pulls away slightly. "You want the first time I fuck you to be in a stairwell, Lennon Rose?" he growls, letting my hands go as he reaches behind me and hoists my skirt up. His rough, calloused fingers squeeze the sensitive flesh of my ass. "Right here, right now?" I whimper as one of his fingers drifts between my legs, and without any fanfare, he slides my thong to the side and spreads the lips of my pussy. The sound betrays me, and I moan with every movement. "God, you're so fucking wet. Is this for me, or is it left over from Damon?"

The tiny gasp I let out makes him chuckle, and he inserts his middle finger into me. My pussy clenches around his flesh, and just as I'm about to say something, he fists the back of my head with his other hand and kisses me again.

I'm gasping as he pulls away, pushing himself into me with each thrust of his finger.

"You didn't answer me, princess. Is this for me, or is it for Damon?" His voice rumbles into my mouth as he adds a finger, going deeper. The way he curves them, the way he uses his thumb to roll over my clit... I can feel myself squeezing him, tightening around him, so close to climaxing.

"You," I whisper, knowing my chest is flushed pink. "And also, Damon."

He smiles. "And Jude? Does Jude make you wet, too?"

I squeeze my eyes shut as his thumb flicks against my clit roughly. Thinking about Jude in the bathroom, thinking about the way his come tasted on my lips, or the way it would feel to fuck him with that piercing...

The way it would feel to fuck all of them at once.

"I don't know," I answer. "I–I like all of you–"

He bends down and plants a kiss behind my ear. I can tell from his breathing that he's a live wire, too. If I could just unbuckle his pants...

"I'm not going to make you choose, Lennon," he says roughly. "If you want one of us, you get all of us." His words cause my body to shudder and clench around his fingers, and he groans as I hear him unzip. "Fuck it. If I go one more day without feeling your tight little pussy, I'm going to explode."

I nearly cry with relief as I throw my head back, scraping my scalp against the hard wall.

"Lennon," Silas hisses, his hands gripping me hungrily. His mouth presses against mine, and I can feel the fervent need in every movement. His tongue sweeps back into my mouth, and he pulls back as he removes his fingers, sticking them into his mouth and smiling monstrously as he sucks on them. "You taste like fucking honey."

I moan as he works to pull my skirt up and my thong to the side again, tugging at the leather material and hoisting me up against the wall.

Anyone could walk in and see us. Anyone could catch us here just like this.

With my back against the concrete wall, and Silas driving into me...

I cry out as the warm head of his cock presses against my opening. I can't see it very clearly, but I can tell it's thick. He groans as he pulls away, and I pant as I wait for him to thrust into me fully. His strong fingertips grip my thighs and ass firmly, and I move my hips over the top of his shaft.

"I should be a gentleman and ask about birth control," he mutters below my ear before leaving a wet kiss there.

I shake my head quickly. "IUD."

"Good girl," he purrs, teasing my entrance. "Look what you've made me do." I'm breathing heavily, clawing at his shirt, anything to get his cock inside of me. I've never needed sex like this before—never felt this voracious and fervent. "You wear that little skirt all morning, and then you open up to me..." He kisses my neck, biting the sensitive skin roughly as he presses his thick shaft against my pussy. "But then I felt how wet you are—how *tight* you are... I'm going to lose my mind if I'm not inside of you soon."

"Oh my God," I breathe, frustrated. "Just fuck me already, Silas."

I have to give him credit, he looks surprised at that. I give him a coy, little smile, and something dark passes over his face. It's then that I realize I used my commanding voice from high school.

It sets him off.

Thrusting into me, I cry out as he sheathes himself all the way, giving me no time to get used to his size, his length. I hiss, the burning soon giving way to a fullness I've never experienced. I feel myself stretch around him, and the feeling is exquisite.

"Oh, God," I whimper, and he pulls all the way out before driving back into me. I can feel the wall scrape against my back with every movement.

"I like it when you boss me around," he says roughly, his voice uneven and hoarse. I open my lips to respond, but he places a hand over my mouth. "It brings me back to the good old days." He's in so deep as he speaks that I gasp into his hand. "But now it's my turn to boss *you* around."

Fire explodes inside of me as he thrusts into me harder. Ten seconds in, and I can already tell that I'm going to be sore tomorrow.

He begins to pound into me with the tempo of a very

hungry man—a very hungry man who is now feasting on his chosen prey.

I'm no longer the one in control, I've relinquished it to Silas fucking Huxley.

And he's not going to be gentle with me.

This is ten years' worth—a lifetime's worth—of tension.

He's fucking me and getting his revenge at the same time. Perhaps it won't always be this way, but today? Today, he is showing me just how much he's in control now.

His hand comes up to my nipples, now rock hard and peeking through my thin tank top. He rolls one between his thumb and forefinger, and as he does, I feel myself clench around his shaft.

"That's it," he says, baring his teeth and making a low sound in the back of his throat. "You're going to come for me, Lennon Rose."

I shake my head.

He squeezes my nipple harder, and I cry out as my back arches. He continues to hammer me, hitting my cervix and scraping my back with every upward movement. I can feel myself flutter against him, feel myself grip onto him as the first wave of my climax plows through me unexpectedly. I move my hips with his, the sound of our arousal loud in the narrow stairwell. My hair sticks to the back of my neck, and my thighs begin to burn as the rest of my orgasm slowly moves through me.

"Fuck, Lennon," he hisses. "I can feel you milking my cock."

I close my eyes and he slows, extending the pleasure coursing through me, drawing it out of every muscle, every nerve ending. I'm spasming as he stops completely, and if I weren't seeing stars, I would look down. I know he's going to come, too. All I can manage to focus on is his face—mouth open, eyes hooded. His tongue hits his cheek and his eyes narrow as I feel him empty into me, his cock pulsing and dancing inside of me, expanding ever so slightly and turning into a steel rod. A slow, deep sound rumbles through him, and he twitches against my body, sighing as his forehead rests against mine once he stops.

He lowers me immediately, and before I can say anything, he drops to his knees and licks me down there, cleaning me up and wiping his mouth as he stands. My lips fall open, and I sag against the wall as he zips himself up. My legs are still shaking, and Silas smirks as he holds a hand out.

"Shall we?"

I nod weakly, knowing I'll never be able to have normal sex again.

thirty

Lennon

By the time Silas drops me back at my apartment, I have just enough energy to shower and brush my teeth before I sleep the rest of the afternoon off. When I wake up, I have fifteen minutes before I need to be at work, so I quickly straighten my hair and apply a bit of makeup. Pulling on a pair of ripped jeans and a baggy black t-shirt, I grab my black booties and purse before heading down the stairs.

No one is at Savage yet, which is probably a good thing. I'm still trying to wrap my head around the last twenty-four hours.

The trip to New York, the back seat with Damon, the apartment with Silas...

And they want me to *move in* with them? I hardly know them—not really, anyway. Our families raised us in this same suffocating town, but that doesn't make us the same. They have rivalries, enemies, and they do some really bad things–like drugging people and tattooing them against their will. That's the kind of stuff you can go to jail for.

No, I need my own place first.

A space to get my bearings.

I sit behind the desk and log into the scheduling program, my eyes roving over the schedule for the night. In the two weeks since I've been working here, I have yet to see a break in their nights. They are *busy*, and their clientele are chomping at the bit to be tattooed by them. When I log into their Instagram account, I see nearly two-thousand more followers since earlier this week. I squint at the screen, going through their old photos, when Jude walks into the studio.

"Hi," I say without looking up.

"Why are you looking at the phone like you're about to throw it against the wall?"

I huff a laugh. "You guys gained nearly two thousand new followers recently. I'm just trying to figure out why..."

Jude walks around to my side of the desk, taking my phone from me as he scrolls through the account. He makes a tsking noise and hands it back, and my mouth drops open at what I see.

"Church of the Rapture?" I whisper, looking at the post. It's a picture of the front of Savage Ink, and below it...

"But each person is tempted when he is lured and enticed

by his own desire. Then desire when it has conceived gives birth to sin, and sin when it is fully grown brings forth death."

Jude nods. "That's the one. Those new followers? They're *hate* following us."

A shiver works down my spine. "What does that mean?"

Jude snorts, walking away. His dark grey shirt and black slacks hang off his muscular body perfectly, and from behind, his tousled hair is nearly copper in the warm light. He turns to face me, taking a swig from his water bottle.

"It means there are now two thousand more psychos keeping tabs on us."

My blood cools, and I set the phone down. "That's creepy as fuck," I whisper. Before I can ask why a bunch of zealots care about our little shop, Silas walks through the front door. His eyes instantly find mine, and my stomach flutters as his gaze glides over my casual outfit.

"Lennon," he says, giving me a knowing smile. "You look nice."

Jude snaps his eyes to Silas, and I hide my smile behind my hand as I fake a cough. I don't have time to answer him before Damon is walking through the front door.

He winks, and I turn into a puddle in my seat.

I am royally fucked.

"Lennon noticed we got a bunch of new followers," Jude mentions casually. "Rapture freaks."

Silas stiffens. "Oh?"

"Yeah," I answer, sitting up and walking over to him.

I show him the post, and his eyes scan the words before he sighs and hands it back. "He's just trying to rile us up."

"But why? What happened–"

"Did you get settled with your things?" Silas asks, his eyes boring into mine.

Fine.

I nod. "Yep. If you're lucky, maybe I'll bring some cupcakes tomorrow. Made with love by Betsy."

Jude chuckles on the other side of the studio, and I glare at him. "Betsy?"

"My mixer," I add, twisting my lips to the side as I sit back down. "I promise they won't be vanilla."

Silas's eyes find mine at that, and they burn with an intensity that makes me clench my legs together.

You're going to come for me, Lennon Rose.

I look away as my phone vibrates in my back pocket. I pull it out and answer Lola's text about the apartment. Apparently, someone is planning on moving in this weekend. I furrow my brows as I reply, wondering where the hell I'm going to go if I don't find a place soon.

The night carries on normally, though I do notice a few people peeking into the window periodically. Shivering, I give them all my best scowl as I continue making appointments for the guys through the end of the year. I sincerely hope they don't plan on taking a vacation at any point, because they're all booked up. I remember to text Mindy and ask if she wants to meet for coffee tomorrow morning, and then I stalk the Instagram account of Church of the Rapture. These guys are total nutjobs, and I feel sick when I think about how I danced with Liam a couple of weeks ago.

Silas is wrapping up his station, and I stand to leave. I'm still tired from missing out on last night's sleep, so I say goodnight, walk upstairs, and fall fast asleep.

thirty-one

Damon

We lock up, and I climb into Jude's car. Silas is staying back to do a design for a client. I turn the music off as we drive to the house, and Jude clears his throat when we stop at the main light in town.

"We have to tell her," he says slowly, his hands gripping the wheel tighter. "She could be in danger."

I chew on the inside of my cheek. "Nah. Liam wouldn't fuck with her unless he really had something on us that he could use as collateral, or had a death wish."

"So you think their post today was just a coincidence?" he asks incredulously, his jaw feathering.

I sigh and lean back into the leather seat. "I don't know, man. Why now? We've been in Greythorn for nearly two years."

"Yeah, I guess. I just don't trust any of them." Jude accelerates as the light changes to green. "I guess I'll have to do some digging." I hum in agreement. "Are we going to talk about what happened this morning?"

I smirk and look over at him. "Which part?"

Jude frowns, his brows furrowed as his hands grip the wheel. "You know which part." He glances over at me for a second before facing forward again. "In the back seat? Really?"

I look out the window, trying to hide my smile. "Would you have approved if it were in the bathroom at the house?"

Jude clenches his jaw. "Fuck you, man."

I sigh. "Are you asking because you're jealous? You want her all to yourself?"

He's quiet for a minute. "No. I've just never... shared anyone."

I huff a laugh. "Poor, little rich Vanderbilt, never had to share anything in his life–"

"It's not like that, and you know it," he growls. "If you fuck her, and Silas *wants* to fuck her..."

"Silas *did* fuck her," I add, laughing. "They were making googly eyes at each other all night."

Jude pulls into our driveway and cuts the engine. His hands are still on the steering wheel, the tips white as he grinds his jaw.

"So, what... we're all going to keep fucking her?" He turns to face me, and I have to adjust myself because my dick stirs in my pants at the thought.

"One of us, all of us..." I trail off. "I don't see a problem." Jude opens his mouth, but I cock my head. "It's not like you and I have never fucked around."

Jude's gold eyes bore into mine. "I told you, that was–"

"Why are you so scared of admitting you liked it?" I reach out and caress his jaw, but he slaps my hand away. "There's enough to go around, Vanderbilt." He looks down as he digests my words. I open the door on my side. "Just think about it."

"Silas would never go for it," he admits, looking up at me.

I shake my head. "You'd be surprised."

thirty-two

Lennon

The rest of the week goes by quickly. Wednesday morning, Mindy and I meet for coffee. I tell her all about my hunt for an apartment, and she says she'll keep an eye out. I doubt anything will come of it, but it's nice to know that both her and Lola are looking out for me. I even manage to get Lola to join Mindy and I for drinks on Sunday night, luring her away from the party at the guys' house. Lucky for me, I don't see Liam at The Queen's Arms, and I also manage to avoid being alone with any of the guys.

It's not that I don't want something to happen with them... it's just that I'm confused. I like *all* of them in different ways. Silas, with his brooding, sensitive soul. Damon, with his wild, voyeuristic charm. And Jude, with his silent, otherworldly intrigue... All three offer me something different in how they make me feel. I wasn't even sure I could choose if I had to.

I spend Monday morning hunting for apartments again, having completely ignored Silas's proposition of having me move in. Today officially marks one month since being in Greythorn, and even though I've known all three of them most of my life, I still wouldn't feel comfortable living with them.

But I also can't stay where I am...

No word from my mother, thank God. I swallow the ache in my throat every time I think of her and what happened a couple of weeks ago. Everything she said, the words that will surely haunt me for months or years. I just keep telling myself that I will find a place soon, and then I can figure out my next steps.

By the time I walk down the stairs at six, I'm antsy to see the guys. I didn't see them at all yesterday, but they added me to a group chat last week, so we've all been in contact. Just in the last week, they've really made me feel like a part of the group. I swallow thickly as I unlock the door to Savage, thinking about how somehow, I found my tribe, my *real* friends. Even Mindy and Lola feel like the real deal.

Maybe coming to Greythorn wasn't the worst idea ever, then.

I am just getting settled in my chair when my phone rings, and the name on the caller ID makes my heart pound against my ribs.

Wright.

I frown at the screen and wait for him to go to voicemail.

Two weeks ago, I would've answered. I maybe even would've believed whatever he was going to tell me, whatever lie he had concocted. But right now? I'm just pissed off. I go into his contact details and block him, and then I delete his voicemail without listening.

Growth.

Smiling, I hide my phone in the drawer of the desk.

The night seems to drag on, and every few minutes or so, one of the guys catches my eye. First, it's Silas, and I have to look away from his tight, dark blue shirt as he winks at me, pulling his latex gloves over his strong hands. Then it's Damon as his hand trails across the back of my chair when he walks over, asking about his next client. I have to close my eyes and shake my head to get myself back in the mindset of *working.* Last, it's Jude, who watches me from the corner of the studio, his tousled, copper hair hanging in front of his forehead. I can feel his eyes on the back of my neck.

I am in trouble, but I'm not even sure that I care.

My phone buzzes in the drawer, but I don't check it for the rest of the night. Wright can go fuck himself for all I care, and I don't want to hear what he has to say. I'm sure he figured out a way to contact me from another phone. I might have to change my number, because I never want to speak or hear from him again.

I'm sitting on Jude's chair when the door jangles at nearly two in the morning. I locked it after the last client left, and we're all drinking beer and talking about the cake I brought in a couple of days ago. My eyes fly to the person standing outside, and I drop the glass bottle on the concrete floor when I see the familiar face watching me in the dark.

"Who the fuck is that?" Damon asks, setting his bottle down and standing.

I'm too stunned to speak. I stay frozen, ignoring the broken glass all over the floor.

"Lennon," Silas says sternly.

I clear my throat and look at him. "It's Wright. My ex."

"Well, shit," Damon says, a smile playing on his lips.

"What is he doing here?" I hiss, just as Wright knocks on the door.

"Lennon? Can we talk?" he asks from behind the glass. He's wearing a suit, because of course. He's never *not* wearing a suit, except when he's at the gym. I don't even think he owns a pair of jeans.

"We can tell him to leave," Jude suggests, his eyes on Wright.

What the hell is he doing here? How did he find me?

"No, it's fine." I look down at the glass. "Sorry, I'll clean that up."

"On it," Damon says before I can move, quickly heading to the closet.

I'm too distracted to thank him as I walk to the door, unlocking it and holding it open for my ex-fiancé.

"What are you doing here?" I ask on a sigh, reluctantly letting him inside.

"Me?" He storms in, twisting around to face me as

the front door swings shut. "What the hell are *you* doing here?" He looks behind me at the guys.

"I work here." Crossing my arms, I take a step back. "How did you find me?"

He runs a hand through his short brown hair. "I've been trying to call you all day, Lennon."

I look behind me, and without another word, Silas directs the guys into the back alley to give Wright and I some privacy. Damon scoops the last of the glass up with the broom before following Jude and Silas out.

I spin around to face Wright again. "Why have you been trying to call me?"

He reaches out for my hands, but I pull them away, taking another step back.

"I–I'm sorry. Okay? I realize I look like a complete ass–"

"Yeah, you do."

My words startle him. I never talked back before, never pushed against his ideals and his gaslighting. I just took everything in stride without question.

But not anymore.

"Lennon, I'm so sorry. What happened with Darcy was a mistake. It was stupid. I had cold feet, and I didn't realize how much I missed you until my life started falling apart."

"Her name is Darcy?" I question, tilting my head.

He looks down and thumbs his lip. "I broke it off with her this morning."

The words and insults, along with the anger and fury, I've been keeping inside dissipate instantly at his words.

"Why?" I ask, my voice quieter than I intended. I clear my throat and stand up taller.

"Because I miss you."

His words rock through me, causing my heart to speed up. "You said you didn't realize how much you missed me until your life started falling apart..." I trail off.

He sighs, pleading with me. His eyes are wide, and his face is anguished. If only he'd felt this much remorse a month ago.

"I know you came and got your stuff," he says slowly, reaching for my hands again. This time I let him take them. "And like clockwork, things started falling apart. I got sent on a leave of absence from the firm–"

"A leave of absence?"

He nods. "I dropped the ball on a case we're handling. Almost lost us the client." His blue eyes narrow on mine. "I was distracted. I couldn't stop thinking about how empty the kitchen looked without your stupid stand mixer."

I pull my hands away from his, closing my eyes. "I'm sorry about your client, but I don't–"

"It wasn't just the client," he interrupts, taking a step forward and brushing a piece of loose hair behind my ear. I move his hand away, but he doesn't seem to care. "Weird things started happening. My clocks started going on the fritz. My thermostat started blasting heat in the middle of a heat wave, and nothing is where I remember it."

I narrow my eyes. "Like what?"

He sighs. "My razor. It's in a different drawer. As are my other things. Magazines for this religious group started coming, and I get like five emails a day from them. My boxers all have their tags cut out. One of them even has a hole in the crotch, like someone cut a hole out intentionally." I stiffen, and Wright continues. "There's a ticking sound coming from somewhere, and I've torn the apartment apart looking for it, but no matter where I look, it always seems to be coming from underneath my bed–except it's not there," he finishes, panting. His forehead is beaded with sweat. "You wouldn't mess with me like that, right? I'm just going crazy?"

He sounds panicked, desperate. I have to actively try to hide my smile. "No. I'm not that smart."

He laughs as if he agrees. "Okay, good. There are other things too, but it's like every aspect of my life is going haywire without you, Lennon." His eyes are frantic. "I need you back, baby. I'm so sorry for hurting you."

I'm too shocked to speak, so I just open and close my mouth a few times until a word comes tumbling out of my mouth.

"No."

His face pales. "No?"

I cross my arms again. "I don't want you back. We're done."

His eyes bore into mine, and a small part of me wavers under his intense scrutiny. It reminds me of when I rejected Noah, how his ego overshadowed everything.

Wright has the same look of incredulousness on his face right now.

"What do you mean, we're done? You're my fiancé," he corrects me, his voice a little firmer now.

"I was," I say softly, trying to reason with him. "But then you fucked Darcy–"

"Lennon, please–"

"I caught you fucking her from behind in your *office*," I hiss. "I'd come to drop off your favorite cookies since you'd had a hard week at work, and there you were, bending her over your desk."

My eyes sting as I fight back the tears. It hurt like hell, seeing him like that with someone else. A real blow to the ego. I reacted instantly and went back to our penthouse, packed a bag, and got my bearings at a motel in Washington Heights for a few nights before deciding I needed to be at home.

No, not needing to be at home—being *forced* home, because my credit card was declined. All thanks to the man before me.

The anger from earlier makes a comeback.

"I don't want anything to do with you," I hiss, swiping at my face. "Please leave."

His jaw ticks as he takes in my words. Standing straighter, he shakes his head.

"And where will you go, Lennon? Who are these guys, and why are you working here?"

"I'll be fine." I ignore his questions, wanting him gone before I explode.

"What, working in a shithole like this?"

"Hey, man," Silas interjects from behind me. "I think it's time for you to go."

"He was just leaving," I say, crossing my arms as I feel Damon and Jude's presence behind me, too.

"What the hell happened to you, Lennon?" Wright asks, looking at me with disgust. He eyes my outfit of leather leggings and a ripped grey t-shirt, with black studded sandals. "This isn't you. I don't know what kind of life you're trying to chase–"

"My life," I say a little too loudly. "My *real* life."

Wright laughs, mocking me. "Your real life? Working in a tattoo shop, trying to be something you're not? The Lennon I knew went to bed at nine, wore pearls and flats, and read newspapers. You never had an ornery bone in your body."

My cheeks heat, and I grind my teeth together. "That's not true. You just never bothered to get to know me."

"I'm sure," he grits out, eyeing me up and down. "I made a mistake coming here. It doesn't matter what lifestyle you mold yourself into, you'll always be the same boring person, won't you?"

His words shock me to my core, the hurt rolling through me. I clench my fists at my sides and narrow my eyes, opening my mouth to tell him off, when Damon walks up to Wright and shoves him backward.

"Leave. Now," he orders, pushing him toward the door. "And if you ever come back, I promise not to be so gentle," Damon grits out, shoving him once more.

"Get your fucking hands off of me," Wright says,

pulling out of Damon's grip. He looks back at me. "You're making a mistake, Lennon."

Something inside of me snaps at his words. Maybe because they're so similar to the words my mother spoke to me, and maybe I'm sick of people assuming what's best for me. Wright especially. He never knew me, and he never will know me. I cock my head and cross my arms.

"Wait," I blurt, holding a hand up. Wright has the audacity to look relieved, so I give him a wicked smile as I look at Damon. "Lock the door."

Damon's eyes dance with mischief as he reaches behind Wright and locks him in.

"What the hell are you–" Wright asks, but before he can finish the sentence, Damon has his hands behind his back. He leads him to the back room, where I see both Silas and Jude looking way too smug for their own good. "Lennon, what the hell is going on?"

I put my hands on my hips as Damon forces Wright into one of the tattoo chairs. Jude grabs a zip tie and ties Wright's arms and legs together as he thrashes against them.

"Welcome to the dark side of Savage Ink," I say smoothly, winking at Wright as Silas forces him to lay down in the chair.

thirty-three

Lennon

"What the fuck does that mean?" Wright asks, and before he can ask any more questions, Silas slaps a piece of duct tape over his lips. His muted scream is satisfying, and Damon chuckles as Wright thrashes harder against the zip ties.

I look over at Silas, and he's watching me with a mischievous expression. "So? What should we do?" he asks, and when I look at Jude and Damon, they're both waiting for me to give them directions. The thrill of the power I hold makes me smile.

I walk over to Wright and pull the tape off his mouth. He grimaces and pants, glaring at me with pure hatred.

"What the fuck, Lennon," he growls, jerking against the plastic ties that are holding him down. "Let me go. This isn't funny."

I cock my head. "I don't think we should tattoo his forehead," I remark carefully, and his eyes widen.

"What the hell are you talking about?" He looks at Silas. "My father can send you to jail for a very, very long time. Aggravated assault. Look it up and let me go, asshole."

Silas walks around to where I'm standing, placing an arm around my waist. "I do as she says," he answers smoothly. "After all, she's the one you hurt. Not me."

Wright's eyes fly to Silas's arm around his waist. "Are you serious right now?" he asks, looking up at me. "You're fucking him, aren't you?" He laughs cruelly, trying to twist out of the zip ties. Lips curling away from his teeth, he narrows his eyes at me. "When did you turn into such a slut?"

For the second time tonight, his words pierce my chest and make it ache. I swallow and lift my chin slightly, ready to bite back with a mean response, when Damon walks over to me, running a finger down my arm. Goosebumps erupt along my skin and I visually shiver.

"She's not just fucking him," he says sensually, his finger running down the side of my body. I close my eyes and let out a low moan, forgetting Wright's words as Damon's finger trails down my thigh.

Wright laughs again, pulling me out of my stupor. "Funny, isn't it? I could barely get you to fuck me, but you have no problem fucking these losers."

I look down at him, an idea suddenly forming in my mind. "*Funny, isn't it?* You were never able to make me come, but none of them seem to have that problem," I mock.

His nostrils flare, and he looks away. "You're all talk, Lennon. It's so dull."

The corners of my lips curl up. My teasing did the trick. He never did believe me, whether it was opening a bakery or leaving him. He acted as if he controlled my every movement, as if ten years together meant he was entitled to me and my thoughts. Of course, his ego the size of Manhattan couldn't allow him to see the truth.

But I could show him.

Reaching around to Silas, I twist in his arms and pull his neck down, slamming my lips against his. He groans, nibbling my lower lip as he pulls my middle into his hardening cock. When I pull away, I smirk at Wright. Instead of saying anything else, I pull my shirt over my head, exposing the hot pink lace bra.

Thank God I chose cute underwear...

"Still think I'm dull?" I ask Wright, backing up into Silas and reaching behind me to cup his massive erection.

Wright looks at both of us disapprovingly. "What, you're going to enact revenge by fucking this guy in front of me?" He's trying so hard to sound unaffected, but I can hear the strain in his voice–the trepidation.

I shake my head. "No. I'm not going to fuck him." I look at Jude and Damon. "I'm going to fuck all three of them."

Damon and Jude both look at me with raised eyebrows, but the shock wears off quickly as Damon walks over to Wright and slaps another piece of tape over his mouth.

"I'm sick of your voice," he says, his voice low. Wright's eyes widen, and Damon pats him on the top of his head. "Be quiet as we fuck the shit out of your ex-fiancé, or we will actually find a very inconvenient place to tattoo you."

Jude grabs a beer from the fridge and hands it to me, since he must see how my hands are shaking. He's watching me with furrowed brows.

I drink half the bottle before setting it down, instantly grateful for him, for all of them. When I look between them, they're all watching me with determined expressions, waiting for my next move. My stomach flutters with a mix of excitement and trepidation as I realize what I'm about to do—what *we're* about to do. Glancing one more time at Wright, I reach behind me and unclasp my bra, relishing in Wright's groan of disapproval.

I know this is going to haunt him forever—just like the image of him fucking Darcy is going to haunt *me* forever.

Tit for tat—except, instead of a tat, it's going to be three guys fucking me at once.

I ignore the way all three guys are watching me hungrily and chug the rest of my beer. I will need some sort of liquid courage, something to relax me. When my pulse has calmed somewhat, I walk over to Wright. His eyes scan my chest, my taut, peaked nipples. He always loved my breasts, so this show is for him.

To rub it in his face, to make sure he always remembers his inadequacies.

I could not have thought of a better revenge.

"Silas," I say, willing my voice not to shake. "Behind me." I look over my shoulder at him, and something nonhuman looks back—something feral. His icy blue eyes are dark navy, his lids hooded as he slowly walks up behind me, pressing his bulging shaft into my ass. I grab his hands and place them on my tits, watching as Wright thrashes against his tied arms and legs, yelling something behind the tape.

"Twist them," I whisper, taunting Wright. "Hard."

Silas does as he says, and I moan, arching my back into him, squeezing my eyes shut. His calloused fingers are rough against the delicate flesh of my nipples, and the mild pain sends sparks flying to my clit. Everything between my legs begins to pulse with anticipation.

Jude walks to the other side of the table, bending over so that he can kiss me, so that Wright can feel the weight of him on the chair. His mouth claims mine, and he pulls my face into his with his hands just as Silas rolls my nipple between two fingers roughly.

I cry out into Jude's mouth, and Wright screams from behind his tape.

"I thought I told you to be fucking quiet," Damon growls before kneeling in front of the chair and pulling my hips toward his face. I gasp as his stubble scratches the flesh on my stomach, and then I feel his warm hands pulling at my leggings. I step out of my shoes and kick them under the chair, and Damon murmurs something unintelligible when he sees my matching pink thong.

Something electric pulses through me as Jude kisses my neck, pulling me forward so that I'm resting a part of my weight on Wright. When I look down at him, he's watching me with pure hatred.

"How should we fuck you, princess?" Silas asks from behind me, cupping my breasts.

His words send a jolt to the spot between my legs, and I whimper as he squeezes my nipples again. Damon's mouth trails along the flesh of my stomach, and his hands are gripping the back of my ass. I close my eyes and let the sensations take over—of Jude's mouth on my collarbone, of Damon's mouth inching closer to my pussy, of Silas thrusting against my ass as he plays with my aching breasts...

Am I really going to do this? It's not like I don't trust them. If anything, they have proven themselves trustworthy time and time again. And it's not like I haven't crossed the line with all of them—Jude at the party, Damon in the car, and Silas in the stairwell. There's already a precedent.

I look at Jude. "You," I say, my voice uneven.

My skin is tingling from the beer, and I can smell the soap Jude uses in the shower as he pulls away and walks over to the couch. It's like he can read my mind. He sits down as Damon turns Wright's chair to face us.

"Watch as we give her everything you never could," he commands.

Wright's eyes are two black pools of loathing. *Good.*

I walk over to Jude, placing one knee on either side of his legs. I want him inside of me—I *need* to feel his piercing. I haven't stopped thinking about it since that night. I bend down and kiss him, our tongues sliding against each other as his hands come back around to my ass. He slides my cunt up and down his swollen length, and I'm panting by the time he pulls away, looking over my shoulder. I follow his gaze, my eyes landing on Damon.

"You too," I say, my voice throaty.

"Lennon," Jude warns, gripping my ass even tighter. "Are you sure?"

I nod, rolling my hips. I love the way his eyes roll to the back of his head every time I move against him.

"And I want Silas in my mouth," I add, pointing to the back of the couch. "Right here."

Wright makes some sort of defeated sound, and I grin as Damon comes behind me. I realize suddenly that because the light is on, anyone walking by could see exactly what's happening. It's nearly three in the morning, so the chances are low, but it still spurs me on nonetheless. I groan as Damon's large hands come to my ass. He stands behind me, rubbing in circles, pulling me into him ever so subtly. I fist Jude's shirt and close my eyes.

I didn't realize it until tonight–how badly I wanted this.

Them. All three of them.

Us.

My clit throbs on top of Jude, and my stomach flutters with butterflies as I look over at Wright.

Should my first time with them be in front of him?

I'm not in love with him anymore, and I'm really not sure I ever was at this point. He hurt me—ruined my life... but on the other hand, I have him to thank for Silas, Damon, and Jude. Without his cheating ass, I wouldn't be here.

Still... he *hurt* me.

And nothing about coming here has been normal.

In fact, just knowing he'll be watching me as I come undone, just knowing anyone could walk in front of the studio at any moment...

Yes. I want this.

All of this.

Silas comes to stand in front of me. He's carrying a bottle of something I recognize instantly, handing it to Damon over my shoulder.

Fuck. This is really happening.

"Lennon," Jude purrs, fingering my underwear. "Did you wear these for us?"

No.

Yes.

I nod, swaying my hips on top of him.

"Have you ever done this?" Damon asks, rubbing my ass cheeks gently. I know what he's implying. Nervous butterflies flutter through me. I've always wanted to try it.

"No," I answer, looking at Wright. He rolls his eyes and looks away.

"That's too bad," he responds slowly. "Such a pretty little ass, princess," he growls into my ear from behind me.

Jude is breathing shallowly beneath me, so I bend down and kiss him—long and hard. He grabs my panties and rips them off. I gasp as he throws them off to the side, landing on Wright's chest.

"A parting gift," Jude taunts, smirking at Wright. "Doesn't her cunt smell divine?"

Wright growls under his tape. "He wouldn't know," I muse. "He hardly ever went down on me." Jude shakes his head, clicking his tongue.

I look up at Silas and reach for his pants. He chuckles, taking my hand and rubbing his hard erection beneath his jeans.

"Look at what you do to me, Lennon," he remarks, his voice hoarse. "You're going to suck my cock, and then I'm going to fill your pussy with my come."

I whimper as Jude unzips his pants. "That's it," he whispers, freeing his shaft. I nearly forgot about the piercing—the Jacob's ladder. That's what it's called. I googled it after that night.

"This will feel different, but I promise it'll be worth it," he murmurs into my ear. "Trust me." He rubs the thick head of his cock, wet and glistening with pre-cum, against my clit. I look down at him, his gold eyes nearly black as he teases my entrance. "Ready?" he asks, and I hiss as his head slowly slides in. I nod, and he must've needed my confirmation because a second later, he slams into me, and I nearly see stars as I cry out loudly.

thirty-four

Jude

I clench my jaw and slam into Lennon, gritting my teeth as she stiffens on top of me, her back arching as she takes me in fully. Whether or not she was actually ready, I'll never know, but the sound coming from deep inside of her is purely animalistic, so I must be doing something right. Fuck, the way her pussy grabs onto my cock, the way it *milks* me as I hold her down, letting her get used to the piercings and the size, I've never felt anything like it. I could come just being inside of her pussy, just feeling the way she pulses around me, her eyes flaring with delight as I hold her still.

Fuck. Me.

I raise myself onto my elbows, bending my neck so that I can taste her tight, pink nipples. Taking one of them between my teeth, I bite down–not too hard, but enough for her to pulse around my cock again.

Yeah, she could definitely make me come without moving.

Lennon leans forward, and I can tell she's sucking Silas off now, her head bobbing. I pull out of her and slam back in, and she cries out with a mouth full of dick. I try not to smile as I look behind her, at Damon watching me with hooded eyes. He doesn't break eye contact as he drizzles some lube onto Lennon's ass.

"This might sting for a minute," he tells her, unzipping his pants as his dark pink shaft rubs against her smooth skin, oiling it up for her ass.

She doesn't say anything other than some sort of jumbled confirmation. My eyes flick back up to Damon's, and I feel my cock twitch when he enters her, when I feel him slide against the thin barrier separating us.

"Fuck," he hisses, and Lennon whimpers above me, Silas's cock unattended to.

"Hey," I whisper, reaching up for her face. "Breathe. In and out. Slowly," I say, thrusting into her smoothly. I reach down and begin to work her clit, and that seems to help, because with a small snap, I hear Damon fully sheath himself inside of her.

"Oh fuck, oh fuck," she mewls, her mouth a wide 'O'.

"This is so fucking hot," Silas says from above me. I reach up and cup his balls, and he gasps, but he doesn't pull away.

"What the fuck," he breathes, jerking himself as I play with his taut sack.

"Come one, come all," I joke, and Damon chuckles.

"What are you laughing about?" I ask Damon, sliding in and out of Lennon. I'm going to come soon, just feeling Damon's monster cock against mine, knowing he can feel my piercings makes it even harder to hold on. "You weren't laughing when I sucked your cock a couple of months ago."

Lennon mutters something I can't understand. When I look up at her, she's squeezing her eyes shut. When she opens them, I see her look over at Wright.

"Don't look at him," I command. "He can hear you–he can hear *us*. Don't give him the time of day. Just focus on coming all over my cock."

"I'm going to," she whimpers, looking unsure. "I c-can't–"

I slam into her again, feeling how her hot pussy throbs every time that I do. Knowing that with Damon behind her, and me sucking on her nipples... I want to give that motherfucker on the chair a show. I want her to spray all over me.

"Lennon," I direct, just as she takes Silas in her mouth. "Bend backward, toward Damon. Use your hands for Silas."

"But–"

"Just do it," I say sternly.

She sits up straight and tilts herself back a bit, her legs squeezing my thighs so she doesn't fall over. Damon holds her as he slowly moves in and out of her ass.

"God, you feel fucking amazing," he growls.

Lennon reaches out and begins to work Silas with her

hands above me. “Okay, now what?” I grin as I grip her hips, moving my hips *just so* against the wall of her pussy. “Oh–oh–”

I laugh. “Feel different?”

Her chest flushes red instantly, and her body trembles. I play with her nipples as she strokes Silas.

“Fuck,” he hisses, moving into her hands quicker. “I’m going to come,” he says, working faster and fucking her hands, his cock pulling up and hardening.

“Come on her tits,” I order, and he does, emptying out onto them as he groans, low and steady. His shaft jumps as the last of it leaves his body, and I smear it around, using it as lube and twisting her nipples.

“Oh, God,” she cries, arching her back as I cup her breasts and squeeze. “This feels incredible,” she moans out, her voice frayed as it breaks on the last word.

I look behind her at Damon, and his eyes narrow on mine, his bottom lip between his teeth as he thrusts into Lennon.

Jesus.

With every slow thrust, he lets out a sharp breath, and I know he’s getting close. I can tell by the urgency in his movements, the way his hands are gripping her ass cheeks firmly.

“Harder,” she pleads, looking down at me. “Harder,” she repeats, whispering. “I’m so close.”

I do the thing that I know is going to make her come all over me and this couch. I lift my hips slightly and fuck her–hard, fast, and deep. Using one hand, I take my thumb and press down on her clit. Her resulting gasp sounds more like a sob as she rides both Damon and I, chasing her climax. I know she's going to squirt before she does. Her body coils, her pussy is so tight around me that it feels like a steel vise, and then she starts to shake as her eyes roll into the back of her head.

She cries out in gibberish as she sprays my chest, her body convulsing as she drenches me, and I hear Damon swear under his breath as he fucks her through it. I'm going to fucking come soon, feeling her on top of me, hearing the way her wetness sounds against me.

Behind her, Damon moans and meets my every thrust. I can feel his cock harden against mine, against the slick wetness of Lennon's pussy. My balls draw up as my orgasm begins. I let my head fall back against the couch as I growl loudly, feeling myself pour into her with each pulse of my cock. I grip her hips and drive her faster against my rock-hard length.

My breathing is uneven, and I'm still twitching as Damon comes, crying out as his balls slap against her. She slumps onto me, her head on my chest, as Damon pulls out and steadies himself. I lift her off me and lay her down on the couch. We're all still panting, and Silas looks over at Wright. The idiot is still fighting against the zip ties.

"What did you think?" I ask slowly, pulling my pants up as I walk over to him. Ripping the tape off him, he bares his teeth at me. "Do you think she enjoyed it?" I tease, looking back at Lennon lying on the couch like she just ran a marathon. Her chest rises and falls as she watches us. I touch the liquid on my chest, holding it up for him to see. "I hope you took notes."

"Fuck you," Wright hisses, and I chuckle as I look down at him. "What are we doing with him, princess?" I ask, looking back over at Lennon. Silas and Damon are cleaning her up and helping her off the couch.

"I don't care," she says, grinning. "Just get him the fuck out of my sight."

I grab a pair of scissors and snip off the zip ties. Wright jumps up, fists raised, but before he can throw a punch, Damon and Silas grab his arms and drag him out.

"If you ever come near her again," Silas growls, shoving him out of the door, "I swear to God, I will kill you."

Wright looks between the three of us, and he must decide it's not worth it, because he turns and jogs away.

When I look back at Lennon, she's watching me with a sleepy, warm smile.

thirty-five

Lennon

I never knew pleasure like that was possible. I'd never felt that, not even when I touched myself. Not even when I bought the vibrator of all vibrators–the one that sucks and licks and everything in between. This? This was an out of body experience. The orgasm Jude pulled from me, mixed with Damon and Silas... it was potent and almost terrifying that my body was capable of something so large. It was bigger than me. The waves of my climax were almost too much to handle. I thought for sure that I would fly off of Jude's cock and through the ceiling at one point.

Wright is gone, so I get dressed. Honestly, after Jude entered me, I couldn't have cared less about Wright. He fucked up, and I'm glad we gave him a taste of his own medicine. We may face repercussions–he's not against running to daddy for every little thing–but I'll worry about that later. For now, I got my revenge.

And it felt really fucking good.

"I'll walk you home," Damon says, grabbing his phone and keys. "You guys clean and lock up."

I glance over at the couch. It's like someone poured a glass of water over the leather. I feel my cheeks heat just as Damon grabs my hand.

"Hey." He grabs my attention, following my gaze. Bending down, he whispers in my ear. "That was the hottest fucking thing I've ever seen," he says, his voice low and husky.

I swallow. "That–it's never happened before."

Damon smiles and pulls me into his large body. "Well, then it's an honor to witness your first time."

I smile and say goodbye to Silas and Jude. I'm *so* tired all of a sudden, and I know I'll sleep well tonight. Damon opens the door, and we turn right, walking up the stairs to my apartment.

In an instant, I know something's wrong. I hesitate on the landing as my door hangs off the hinges.

"Wait," Damon says, pulling me back. "Go back downstairs and get the guys. I'll check it out."

"No, I'll–"

"Lennon," he growls, his eyes fiery and heated. *Angry.* "Go. Now."

I turn around and jog down the stairs. When I get into Savage, Silas and Jude are still cleaning.

"I think someone broke into my apartment," I

breathe out, my voice frazzled. I'm so tired that I'm beginning to see stars.

They both drop what they're doing, and we head upstairs. Damon is looking through the wreckage when we get inside, and I cover my mouth as I look around. All of the cupboards in the kitchen are open, and all of the drawers are pulled out. My bed is a mess, and all the clothes in my closet are strewn about. Everything is overturned. Whoever did this managed to look in every crevice of the small apartment. Everything appears to still be here, though. At least the things that matter to me, like Betsy.

Goosebumps work up my arms to the back of my neck when I realize this happened while we were all downstairs.

"Who the hell would do this?" I ask, wrapping my arms around myself. When I look up at Silas, his lips are thin and he's looking between Jude and Damon. "Liam," I whisper, remembering his threat.

I'm sorry that you're going to get mixed up in all of this, Lennon.

I look at Silas, narrowing my eyes. "Why would Liam James break into my apartment?"

Silas sighs, running a hand through his dark, golden hair. "I don't know. But they—" He trails off, sighing. "They hate us, and I think they're trying to scare you."

I let out a frustrated laugh. "Scare me? Scaring me would be sending me a weird letter in the mail, not committing a crime by breaking and entering."

"The Church of the Rapture hate us, Lennon," Jude

states, coming around to where I'm standing. "Their network is huge, much bigger than we give them credit for. They have connections. We may act like the bad guys, but I can assure you, we'd never murder anyone–"

"They murdered someone?" The guys all share a look. I'm getting really fucking sick of them hiding shit from me. "Someone better tell me what the fuck is going on," I command, my voice a little louder.

Damon rubs his lips as he looks between Silas and I. "Nothing's been proven." He looks at Silas. "Should you tell her, or should I?"

"Tell me *what*?" I growl, leaning against the small island.

Silas looks me in the eyes, his face anguished. "My parents didn't go crazy, Lennon," he says, looking between Damon, Jude, and me. "They murdered someone."

My mouth falls open. "But you said they were in a psychiatric hospital–"

"They are," he adds, pushing off the wall he was leaning against and walking over to me. "Because Liam got them a plea deal."

"The whole church is fucking crazy," Damon mutters from behind Silas. "The judge on the trial was a member of the church."

Silas nods. "And my parents got off on insanity."

I shake my head. "So they're not locked up, talking to themselves, chained to a bed?"

Silas's eyes burn into mine. "No. They know exactly what they did. It's why we fucking hated having to come back here."

"And why you hate Liam so much," I add, my voice hoarse. I look between the three of them. "So, now what?" I ask, shivering.

Silas points to the bedroom area. "Pack a bag. You're coming to stay with us." I start to argue, but he holds a hand up. "My offer from last week still stands, Lennon. You're not safe here. We'll figure something out, but we need to get out of here." He looks at Damon. "I need you to file a police report." Turning to Jude, he sighs. "And I need you to find out what the hell they think they were doing breaking into Lennon's place."

"How will he find any of that out?" I ask, looking between them.

Jude cocks his head and smiles, putting his hands in the pockets of his trousers. "Because they think they're converting me."

My mouth drops open for a second time. "What?" I screech.

"It's fun," he muses, looking at one of his nails. "I quite enjoy messing with them."

That brings back another memory of tonight. "You screwed with Wright's things," I accuse, smiling.

Jude just clucks his tongue. "Oftentimes, it's the smallest of changes that drives us the most mad. Haven't you ever heard of Charles Manson rearranging his victim's furniture for weeks before he murdered them?"

I shake my head. "You really are a psycho," I concede. Looking at Silas, I shrug. "Okay. I guess I'm moving in with you temporarily. And reluctantly," I add, walking over to my closet and pulling the suitcase down.

"Right," he says slowly, walking over to me and helping me pack the essentials. It feels oddly intimate.

"And then what?" I ask, throwing in a few pairs of underwear, socks, and other clothing items.

"No idea," Silas replies grimly, handing me my toothbrush and toothpaste from the bathroom. "But now that he crossed the line and fucked with you..." he pauses to blow out a breath of air, "it's war."

I finish packing, managing to cram most of my belongings into the suitcase I brought here. Damon offers to carry Betsy, and I grab a few other things strewn about the kitchen. I don't bother cleaning up–the police will want to take a look–but I do look back before closing the door.

I have no idea what this means, or if I should be worried. But Silas is right. I'll feel a hell of a lot better living with them. *For now.* I make a mental note to update my mom on the situation, since it is her property. By the time we get to Silas's house, the lids of my eyes are heavy.

They set me up in one of the guest bedrooms on the other side of the house, the side with Jude's room. I set my suitcase down on the bed, turning to face them as my eyes catch sight of the pink sunrise coming in through the window.

"Now what?" I ask, waiting for them to tell me that everything is going to be okay.

Instead, they each walk over to me and kiss me on the forehead. It's such a juxtaposition from earlier.

"I have no idea," Damon says, and the three of them walk to the door. "For tonight, just get some rest."

And then they leave, closing the door behind them, and I'm left wondering how the hell I ended up here.

I suppose I just have to wait and see what tomorrow brings.

thirty-six

Liam

We get back to my house, and I quickly gesture for the guys to hand me their gloves and shoe covers. I take them out to the back yard and add them to the pile of shit I need to burn, making a mental note to do it tonight in case Silas Huxley decides to play games and name me directly as a suspect. Smiling, I walk back inside and dismiss everyone home for the night. Once they're gone, I pour myself a glass of whiskey and take it outside as I light the pile of evidence on fire.

I feel a tiny bit of remorse for Lennon Rose. I wish she'd made a different choice. It didn't have to be this way. My history with Silas goes back nearly twenty years, and now she's getting caught up in their web of lies and sin. She thinks I'm the bad guy, but it's them infiltrating my church and kidnapping my members, giving them profane tattoos. Kidnapping *me.* My hand flies to my forehead instinctively, and I rub the scar gently.

Sinner.

The bastards had taken such an ugly word and inked it on my forehead nearly two years ago. I'd had it removed as soon as I could, but the scar was there. Silas would always be the scrawny child in my mind, would always have a vendetta against me because of his parents.

And because of one night—one mistake.

I swallow the rest of my whiskey, letting the burn wash away any doubt or remorse in my mind. Setting the glass down on one of my outdoor tables, I close my eyes and think of that night, a new wave of anger flowing through me.

The kiss—and the subsequent rejection.

It was a sin, and I deserved to burn in hell for it. Every time I laid eyes on Silas, I knew he remembered.

And I knew he would use it against me one day, which is why I had to ensure I always had the upper hand. Laying with another man was immoral—and he *knew* how much I hated how tempted I was that night. How much I fought against it for years. How many times I prayed to wake up feeling normal. But Silas knew—he saw right through me. Not only did he injure my pride, but he was set on injuring my status as the leader of the church to get back at me. He would use my greatest sin as his revenge, as his punishment.

But I was going to ensure Silas never had a chance to speak the truth.

Even if it meant silencing him and his friends forever.

TO BE CONTINUED...

You can download Savage Gods, book two of the Savage Hearts series, below:

Savage Gods

Also, don't forget to sign up for my mailing list! There are monthly giveaways, exclusive excerpts, and I share news there before anywhere else! It's the best place to keep in touch with me.

Mailing List

Thank you so much for reading!!

acknowledgments

First, thank you to my TikTok family for begging me to write more books in the Greythorn/Ravenwood Academy world. I did not plan on writing this series at all, but I pushed everything else I had planned for 2022 back because y'all loved these characters so much. Thank you for your support, and for your shares and comments and messages. They mean the world to me. #BookTok #SmutTok forever.

Thank you to Renee and Ashleigh for being my alpha readers for this series. You guys have been so incredibly helpful with suggestions. It really does make a world of difference to have someone read your words as you write them. You both gave me the confidence to keep writing when I felt like parts of this story were utter crap.

Ashleigh, you have been such a lifesaver. Thank you for all of your help organizing my disorganized life. You have been invaluable. I hope we can meet in person one day and talk about romance novels while drinking tea and eating biscuits.

Mackenzie, thank you for the edits! You have a way of keeping my writing and my style my own, while also enhancing certain parts. I have loved working with you.

Dez, thank you for the gorgeous original covers. I can't wait to turn them into hardbacks soon.

Emma, thank you for helping me with the new covers. Your professionalism and quick turnaround was much appreciated, and I know people will love these just as much as the Ruthless Royals duet.

To my Dark Hearts, I love you guys. Thanks for being supportive of me over the years, for encouraging me and for being so enthusiastic.

To my family, thank you for always being so patient while I check out and write. I know working two jobs keeps me far busier than we'd like (props to my husband for holding down the fort). I am so lucky to have all three of you by my side. Hopefully soon I will be writing full-time and won't be so frazzled, lol. Follow your dreams, my loves, because anything is possible! Mummy loves you.

And to my author friends. I am so grateful to have you all in my life, and so proud of what you've accomplished. Keep writing, keep breaking those glass ceilings, and keep being your badass selves. <3

about the author

Amanda Richardson writes from her chaotic dining room table in Yorkshire, England, often distracted by her husband and two adorable sons. When she's not writing contemporary and dark, twisted romance, she enjoys coffee (a little too much) and collecting house plants like they're going out of style.

You can visit my website here: www.
authoramandarichardson.com

Facebook: http://www.
facebook.com/amandawritesbooks

For news and updates, please sign up for my newsletter here!

also by amanda richardson

Love at Work Series:

Between the Pages

A Love Like That

Tracing the Stars

Say You Hate Me

HEATHENS Series (Dark Romance):

SINNERS

HEATHENS

MONSTERS

VILLAINS (coming 2023)

Standalones:

The Realm of You

The Island

Dirty Doctor

Ruthless Royals Duet (Reverse Harem):

Ruthless Crown

Ruthless Queen

Savage Hearts Series (Reverse Harem)

Savage Hate

Savage Gods

Savage Reign

Shadow Pack Series (Paranormal Romance, under my pen name K. Easton):

Shadow Wolf

Shadow Bride

Shadow Queen

Printed in Great Britain
by Amazon

16198375R00150